I WILL

BE OKAY

I WILL BE OKAY

a novel

BILL ELENBARK

Walrus Publishing | Saint Louis, MO 63116

Walrus Publishing
Saint Louis, MO 63116
Copyright © 2020 Bill Elenbark
All rights reserved.
Walrus Publishing is an imprint of Amphorae Publishing Group, LLC

Song lyrics are the copyright of The World is a Beautiful Place and I Am No Longer Afraid to Die, and are used with permission.
http://theworldisabeautifulplace.com

For information, contact:
4168 Hartford Street, Saint Louis, MO 63116
www.amphoraepublishing.com

Manufactured in the United States of America
Cover Design by Kristina Blank Makansi & Elena Makansi
Cover art: IStock, Hand lettering: Elena Makansi
Set in Adobe Caslon Pro and Milo OT
Library of Congress Control Number: 2020933864
ISBN: 978-1-940442-28-0

To Mike. And Elie.

ONE

EXPLOSIONS IN THE SKY send echoing vibrations rattling through the field around Stick and me side by side in the wet tall grass with the heat and the bugs and the sweat, Stick at my side watching the fireworks erupt, one by one then in a sweltering rush with this high and these thick jolting booms crashing through every second with a flash in the distant-splintered darkness like I'm dreaming. Broken dreaming. Fevered images of Stick and me on the grass, sprawled out in the dark, legs splayed gazing up at the lights beaming bright for an instant almost blinding and then fading, flitting fading, disappearing after breaking until I forget that they were there and now they're gone.

The moon is full. Stick noticed and he mentioned it, but he notices things more than me. We're lying in the grass near the edge of my development, set back from the road that snakes by his house, the fireworks swelling over shingled roofs beyond the train tracks, and I forget how we got here, why Stick suggested it—but I keep forgetting things, maybe from the glue. They say huffing is worse than other drugs, but I don't mind, I like the high, and it makes me happy and horny and sleepy at the same time. I close my eyes and find his face inside, his skin against my skin, arms wrapped around mine, this thin, knotted mess of overheated flesh, in my dream fused like freaks until I wake.

A mosquito crawls up my wrist and digs into my hand but it doesn't move when I slam, it squishes into my thumb, sinking into the blood, and I'm tired but not sleepy it's like I'm already sleeping or I'm wide awake and dreaming but I don't remember dreaming and I don't remember anything with this sticky humidity pressing through me like the blood on my skin and Stick's skin on my mind, his fingers outstretched in the grass next to mine, and I inch them closer until the tips are touching. Delicate touching.

"You think your parents would mind if I slept over?"

"What? No," I say but it's too quick, he'll think I'm sick. He's never stayed over my house before.

"It just sucks at home right now, Matt."

Stick hands me the bag with the glue, but I've had enough.

"It's cool," I say, as calm as I can manage. "My mom likes you."

"Really?" He shoots me a wicked grin.

"Not like that!" I slap him and my hand lingers against his chest, soaking up the heat. He lets it linger.

"I hate that I have to work tomorrow," he says. "Fourth of July."

He sits up from the grass with the bag and the glue, crinkling the edges and sticking his face into the center, pulling in the next hit long enough and deep enough to force a cough and then he offers me the bag again. I feel the wet of the grass or the sweat on his skin when he touches me. I take it this time.

"How early do you have to go in?"

"Eleven," he says.

"Oh. You still coming to the party?"

My parents throw a party every Fourth of July—this big blowout barbecue for all our relatives and friends, and since we're Puerto Rican we've got a massive family and it's a massive party, but this is our first year living in this neighborhood and apparently a bunch of the neighbors have people over, too, so it turns into a monster block celebration every summer, Stick told me.

"Yeah, I should be out in time."

The lights in the sky are white now, the colors harder to produce someone told me one time, back at my old school before we moved away from all my friends on the baseball team and everything I'd ever known so Dad could be closer to work. I hated him then—I still hate him now—but I wouldn't have met Stick if we didn't move, so maybe it's fate. Like when the Fourth Hokage sacrificed his life to seal the Nine-Tailed Fox into a baby boy, Naruto Uzumaki, the greatest ninja of all time, 412 episodes into an anime series that I watched every day before Stick.

"Maybe I won't even go in," he says. "I mean, I've been thinking about quitting anyway."

"You just started a week ago!"

"Yeah," he says. "I'm not beat for the working life." He smiles and swipes his hair left to right across his forehead, like he always does, the wispy poof at the side near his eye, the sweat matting it down against the skin. "What about you? Is your dad making you get a job?"

"No, not yet. He's letting it slide for baseball camp."

His face is clear, a little bright off the moon's reflection, and I can see the sweat by his ear slipping down his neck, see his lips blotted and chapped or a little charred from the glue. There's screaming and clapping through the woods by Woodbridge High, and I think about my mother, how we used to watch the fireworks with the teachers from her school and their kids, these blathering girls and smelly boys who didn't bother with me or I didn't bother with them, and I think she dragged my brother to the high school tonight, continuing our tradition at a new school without me. Because Stick.

"When does camp start?"

"Next week," I say. "But I'm trying to get out of it."

"Really?"

"Yeah. I told my mom it didn't make sense to spend all that money on baseball camp when I didn't even play for JV this year but she said they already put a deposit down and I need to talk to my father about it and he just—I mean, I tried. He wasn't listening."

I missed the start of the season after I sprained my ankle and Dad thinks that's the reason I didn't play very much, but the athletes here are bigger than me and stronger than me and a different level of competition than I had at my old school. I spent the spring cheering from the bench.

"So no job and no baseball… what are you planning to do?"

"I don't know," I say. "This."

He glances at me and plays with a smile. "Yeah," he says. "This is nice."

I watch his shaggy hair and his eyes, bright blue like the sky—not this sky, with its moonlit grays and clouds so high you can't see them, not even in the glow of the fireworks, but the afternoon skies with no clouds and no smoke and no buildings, no sounds, just silence through the fields where I played as a kid, all alone but not lonely and lost in the spread of the sky.

"You know, Trevor told me the other day that some jerks from school were asking about us."

"Asking what?"

"You know, whether we're like a couple or something, the way we're always together," Stick says. "Some people think we're gay."

I start to laugh but it doesn't come out, and I want to sink down and hide but there's nowhere to hide and all the sounds are obscured and the colors still blurred and this ridiculous heat won't stop pressing through my skin and it's beginning again, this sickening feeling that keeps coming up and I can't stop it, the way it takes hold and it doesn't let go—these thoughts about Stick—how they keep busting out, like explosions again, high above the trees in a mass of mixing colors, streaming reds and yellows and blues so bright I see Stick in the dark, his face in the light when he looks up at the sky.

"Maybe we don't tell anyone I'm sleeping over."

"Okay," I say.

I pull up the bag and lean forward to take a hit, wrapping the edges around the corners of my mouth and above my nose, a swift rough tug at my throat that surges back like a rusted bolt to my brain, rattling through the crevices and the folds of gray matter at the start of some dream—a seesawing dream soaked in festival sounds, bells and alarms and carnival whistles, loud enough to hear but not quite place the song. Stick shifts forward, sweeping his hair left to right, and the panic queues up like it's about to attack, crack-crack-crack like a whipsaw chain at my back. I have this saying, whenever I get nervous or afraid, almost like my mantra. I will be okay. Everything.

"Have you ever hooked up before, Matt?"

"Huh?"

"Before I met you, were you ever—you know—with a girl?"

I shake my head. The sky is spinning, black and spinning, but our knees are touching, this delicate touching, and I think we're at the climax, at first these smallish bursts over the trees in swift succession, then a barrage of light like lightning strikes above the Hidden Leaf Village, an immortal struggle for the fate of humanity in the hands of one young ninja named Naruto. If I was as brave as him, I'd just plain say it. Tell Stick the truth.

"Not even a blow job?"

He laughs and the panic shifts down my spine through my throat, sharp at the edge, pushing out from inside.

"Staci and me fooled around a bit," he says. "I mean, I told you about that, but I don't know, I haven't really talked to her since school ended. I don't know if I really like her."

I must be thinking out loud and he can hear me, with all this talk about us being gay and being with girls and the way our hands are touching, he's letting me touch him, the tips of my fingers on his skin as I breathe him in and catch a glimpse of his eyes, hoping for a sign. I will be okay, I say, possibly out loud this time.

Then the lights beam bright all at once in the sky, explosions of white with deep reds and spinning blues, and I lift my hand to block out the light, to block all this doubt from messing with my mind, and the sound gets louder now so Stick turns to look and I'm staring at the shaggy waves of brown nestled over his neck, tanned and golden from the summer in the sun. He turns back as the explosions crash through the trees, this chaos behind me, the sound of a horn from the train snaking past our development, piercing through the dark until I slip, I lose my grip and fall into Stick, my hands on his thighs and my head on his chest, collapsing in the heat of his chest. The sweat from his shirt seeps down through my skin, sucking me in, and he pulls me up, sliding my head along his neck, lifting my chin against his chin and my face against his face. I press my lips into his cheek like it's some kind of mistake. But I linger.

I close my eyes so I can't see his eyes and my lips wander down his cheek to his lips and he kisses me back for a second, this sweet wetness on my mouth for a single second, maybe longer. Longer. He pushes me away.

When I open my eyes, he's backing away after pushing me away, but I push forward, knocking his hands away, his arms down to his waist and I lean forward with my face.

And he kisses me, above the chin, missing my mouth then finding my lips, a desperate stab of his tongue through my skin and I can taste it I think but it's all so overwhelming. My eyes are open and Stick is kissing me. We're kissing.

I reach out to pull him closer, my hands around his back but he stops me, pulling away and breaking the kiss. He slips from my grip and scrambles to his feet.

"Stick?"

The noise from the train scrapes into my brain, this booming braking over trembling tracks, racing past so fast it slips into my dream like it's all been a dream but it can't be, I'm awake. And this isn't a dream.

"Matt." Stick's up on his feet, stepping back on the grass in the lights, it's so bright out now with the moon and the train and the explosions overhead, cascading in rhythm. He stumbles backwards.

"I gotta go."

"Wait—"

I try to stand, but my sneakers slip on the grass and Stick speeds into a sprint across the field, rushing away from me. The train clicks past and the horn fades fast and the fireworks stop. Everything stops.

I look up at the sky in the dark with this high and I want to chase after him but I can't really move.

I can't believe he kissed me.

I will be okay. Everything.

TWO

The best part about being a monster
Is not caring what happens to yourself.
Having teeth that can break without breaking.
No one wants to be your friend.

THE WORLD IS A BEAUTIFUL PLACE and I Am No Longer Afraid to Die. The greatest band that ever existed in the history of recorded music. It's pretty obvious to anyone who's paying attention, but most people aren't paying attention. Not to me and not to Stick and not to Stick and me at school, I didn't think, I don't know what Trevor was suggesting, there's no way it's obvious—we don't walk around town in tight jeans and blue hair and we don't have earrings, even though I really want earrings, it's just that it's a pretty big sign and I don't want to give signs, I just want to get through high school without anyone noticing so I press the volume thirty-eight times to blast the rest of the track, The World is a Beautiful Place is never loud enough for me.

I know the name is a bit extra, maybe too emo and not hardcore or punk enough like the hip hop stuff everyone in school loves, but I can't help it, I'm fascinated with the way their songs bounce around in my head, left to right, soft then loud then another level louder with these jangly guitars and whirling percussion, speeding up and up and up like a train down the tracks, this constant building to breaking that spins through your brain when you're fifteen and gay and you finally kissed the boy you're obsessed with, you just haven't heard from him since.

"Matty, what's taking so long? Your father's waiting for you!"

I have The World Is on full blast, bouncing off the tiles around the bathroom, all my thoughts about Stick and our kiss before he left and I stumbled home alone.

"Mateo Luis, are you alive in there?"

Mom knocks on the door in rapid succession, pauses half a second and bangs again. I have issues with taking long showers, even when I was little, before I realized it was the only place I could masturbate without my family interrupting.

"Your father needs help putting up the tent."

Mom gets manic the week of a party, she's on the weather app 24-7, tracking cold fronts and jet streams and quoting rain predictions like she has a degree in meteorology, but I don't think it's supposed to rain so I'm not sure the point of the tent and I don't know what the rush is, it's not even noon and we're on Puerto Rican time which is at least two hours later than normal time for normal people and no one in my family is remotely normal.

"Matty, come on, I have to pee!"

Nico is next at the door, banging on the wood even louder than Mom, and I don't respond to him either, I try not to feed his constant quest for attention. He's three years younger than me but he just turned twelve so it's more like four and I got enough stress with Mom and Dad and school and baseball, I can't deal with my little brother right now. Especially when I'm thinking of Stick.

I texted him this morning like nothing happened, like I haven't been thinking of our kiss every second since he left, my first kiss with a boy, or some kind of god taking on human form in the form of Stick, and I must have been out of my mind to even try, high from all the glue and the fireworks and Stick next to me on the grass, touching my skin. I couldn't resist. I'll be sixteen next year and I'm fully desperate.

Stick's real name is Henry, but nobody calls him Henry, and I get why, it's not a good name and it doesn't fit his face and he's been Stick ever since I met him. Not because he's good with a bat and not for the size of the stick in his pants, not that I have any clue about that, not yet. But Stick is Stick because he's tall and thin, or he used to be tall when he was a kid. He's not much taller than me anymore and he doesn't use his real name.

I have an ordinary name, nothing cool like Stick. Just Matt, short for Mateo, but I hate it when anyone calls me that and they accentuate the accent like I'm from a foreign country, not some boring suburb in Central Jersey. I used to be Matty when I was younger, but I switched to Matt when we moved to Woodbridge, which sounds older and cooler maybe, to Stick. I want to be cooler to him.

You outside yet?

I thought it was Stick so I jumped out quick, wet and dripping on the bathmat. It's just Sammy.

No, I text back.

I need to get my brother's games back, he wants them tonight.

Sammy, who's not really Sammy—it's Sameer but we always call him Sammy—he lives in our neighborhood with his parents and his grandparents who kind of hate us—all the Latino boys on this side of the neighborhood. Sammy says the older generation thinks American kids are a bad influence on him, but I don't know, he smokes more pot than Stick and me combined and he's always talking about getting laid, which okay, they may have a point about America.

Give me an hour, I gotta help my dad with the tent. The World Is continues to ring out from the speaker and I've been testing the limits of its volume controls, every morning in the shower since I got it for my birthday, drowning in the sound of the band's first album. Stick introduced me to them last winter—I still remember what he said, "Wait, you need to hear this"—like stop, drop everything, this is more important than air or water or Fire Style Jutsu—the art of the Magnificent Dragon Flame—and I think I fell in love with him then, downstairs on the scratchy carpet of our basement, The World Is booming out of this speaker, engulfing us like a giant flame. I even stole my mantra from one of their songs and I need it now, freaking out that Stick isn't texting back, drying off on the rumpled bathmat, thinking of our kiss.

I will be okay. Everything.

"Get some goddamn clothes on and come outside," Dad says when I open the door. "Now."

※

My neighborhood is segregated, that's the only way to explain it—to the right is the Latino side and to the left is the Indian section, and near the back around the corner are the rich white families with rear decks and pools instead of cracked patios but they don't really interact with us much, Trevor and Gavin did during the school year but not really this summer. The Latino families are all outside on their lawns, putting up their tents and their tables and red-white-and-blue decorations, salsa music cranked to unnecessary levels from a sound system parked in between us and the Indian side. One of my neighbors has a nephew who's a DJ, this big Dominican dude setting up the equipment— speakers and amps and mixing board and mics—struggling to lift the heavy gear into place.

"Help me with this pole," Dad says.

Some guests have arrived already, parked out on the street leading into the development, past the open field where Stick and I watched the fireworks last night. He still hasn't texted so I know he's upset, and the only thing I can think is to fake it, pretend I was so wasted I don't even remember the kiss. I've thought before that Stick might be gay, the way he doesn't talk about girls too much and the way he lets me touch him, but I couldn't ever ask him, I couldn't risk it.

"Sammy's coming over soon."

"Good. He can help with the tent."

Dad's always pissed when Mom's family comes over. He likes to spread that anger around.

"Come on come on come on, get the connector."

He points to the intermixed pile of metal posts on the lawn, motioning with animation at some specific location but I'm searching as he's straining and he's getting upset that I can't read his mind.

"Oh, for Christ sake," he says and drops the pole to grab the connector. "I need a beer."

I'm not out to my parents yet. I don't even think they suspect. But then I didn't think anyone suspected, and Trevor and Gavin are going around talking about Stick and me maybe, which is annoying. I mean, I'm okay with being gay, but I'm not about joining the Gay-Straight Alliance at Woodbridge High, and I'd rather come out at my own pace, after I've left my father's house. Not that he's homophobic, not outwardly, I'm just not sure how he'd react, and I want to keep it a secret between Stick and me. Just us.

"Let's get this done." Dad returns from inside and sets an open bottle on a folding chair near the sidewalk. "Your mother's parents are already on their way."

We live in Avenel Green, which isn't very green but it is in Avenel, part of the sprawling suburb that is Woodbridge Township, a group of townhouses carved out of the woods between the highway and the train tracks. Nothing much happens here, or nothing all that interesting, not since that woman died in a car crash that split her in half, her top through the windshield splatted onto the pavement, with the bottom still inside, underneath the seat belt. They say she must have worn the restraint hanging off, like some people do, to avoid messing up their shirts or their skirts or their pretty summer tan lines, but I say it must have been some kind of crash to split her in half.

Dad and me aren't really talking, we're just working, setting up the posts and the connectors and slamming the anchors into the grass, wet from the rain and the morning humidity, too loose to hold the posts in place. The Dominican DJ's beats get louder as Dad's beer gets emptier and he finds some concrete blocks from the shed to steady the structure. We pull on the tarp just in time for Mom to come outside.

"You put it here?" she says.

"Yeah. Where the hell were we supposed to put it?"

"I thought on the side," she says, pointing to the edge of the house. "Toward the back."

"It's sloped over there. All the tables would be slanted."

Mom looks over at the grass then back at the tent, the one we're standing underneath, sweaty and frustrated. She sighs.

"Now everyone has to come through the tent to come inside."

"So?"

"That's stupid," she says. "Can you move it?"

"Nope."

Dad's already doing the folding chairs, opening one and motioning for me to assist.

"Matty, you want to help me move it," Mom says, sickly sweet and desperate. She knows he's not going to change his mind and she can't do it herself.

"Matt is busy," Dad says, pulling another beer out of the cooler, but I'm just standing here. In the middle.

Mom waits for a minute, in the silence of the blaring salsa, then she gives up and goes inside "to cook for you like I've been doing all day." Dad doesn't care, he's taking a slug of his beer and setting up the chairs so I step over to help him.

"How's your ankle?" he says.

"It's okay." My ankle's been a mess ever since a nasty slide this spring that caused my shin to buckle and ripped the bones into shattered shards that sliced through every muscle and tendon from my foot to my knee, although the doctor said it was just a sprain. "A little sore but it's okay."

"Are you wearing your compression socks?" He looks across at my bare legs as we unfold the last table.

"Now?"

"No, I mean when you run, dumbass."

"Yeah," I say. I haven't been running that much or doing any of the drills he set up for me, but he's been working late and Mom's been teaching summer school so they don't know. Stick and me have just been hanging out, every day since summer break, sometimes with Sammy but mostly on our own, wandering the streets of Avenel on our bikes, avoiding our families.

"Well, make sure you bring them to camp with your brace in case you need it. I already talked to the coach and he said they're going to see how you respond to a full workload."

"Are you sure I should go? I mean if I hurt my ankle again it would cost me the fall season. Maybe I should rest."

"You've rested long enough."

He finishes his beer and surveys the lawn, the tables askew and the chairs haphazardly placed, the tent sagging in the middle. We're not known for exacting standards in my family.

"I was just thinking of the cost of the camp and all the hours it'll take and maybe I should work instead."

"What the hell are you talking about? You don't want to go?"

"I told you that."

"When?"

I told him two days ago, with the Yankees game blaring, but I guess he didn't listen, or maybe he didn't want to hear. He was on a baseball scholarship when he was in college, before he busted up his knee and gained a lot of weight and never made it back to the team.

"It doesn't matter, you're going. There's a deposit down already and we're not losing it."

"What if I pay you back the deposit from my summer job? It still saves you money in the long run."

That's my only hope to get out of this—to appeal to his aversion to spending money, and I should have thought of this before he signed me up, but it wasn't like he asked if I wanted to play. And that was before I spent three straight weeks alone with Stick. Before we kissed.

"What summer job? You got a job all of a sudden?"

Stick started working as a busboy and I thought I could join him, spend more time with him, skip baseball camp to rest my ankle and spend every waking moment with Stick. Okay that might be a little sick.

"No," I say. "Not yet."

"Are you afraid of playing now or something? That you're going to get hurt again?"

His tone doesn't waver but he's looking right at me, into my eyes, like it's some kind of sympathy, and maybe I should agree because the money thing isn't working and I don't know how to answer, it's not about my ankle and it's not about baseball, not really, I just want to be around for Stick. And I can't tell him that.

"I don't know."

"Well you have to try sometime," he says, stepping forward to reach out, about to tussle my hair like I'm a little kid but he stops and shakes my shoulder, which feels as awkward as it sounds. "You've got a shitload of ground to make up for this season. The only way you'll be a starter in the spring is to do the work now."

I feel a sudden swelling in my throat like I'm about to cry, I don't know why, it's real all of a sudden that the next four weeks will be all about baseball and not about Stick—after the very first kiss with the only boy I've ever liked, before he ran away and hasn't texted all day and maybe after camp he won't even speak to me.

"I have to take your brother to practice," Dad says, heading up the walkway toward the house. "And don't you dare help your mother move this goddamned tent."

THREE

"TE HE ECHADO DE MENOS, MI HIJO."

I don't speak much Spanish. I know I should and I know a little, but I don't speak it in any normal situations and my parents don't either—they were both born here, the United States I mean, New Jersey for my mom and Long Island for my dad, which has its own unique way to communicate but it isn't Puerto Rican. I took Spanish in school this year but it's different than the way my relatives speak, it's more formal and less natural and we spent half the semester on accents instead of common phrases that would help me understand my nana's sister when she hugs me to death and pours out her love in a foreign language.

"How are you, Auntie?"

"Ah you know," she says, no attempt to hide the fatigue in her pause. "Sin quejas sin quejas. Did you eat?"

The party has started, but none of the food is out—my family practices Puerto Rican time for meal preparation as well. The main courses get cooked all day in pots and pans simmering on the stove and in high-backed dishes crowded into ovens and when it's finally ready you wait three more hours because all the adults are too busy drinking or talking to remember the eating and I get so starved at our parties I can literally feel my stomach clawing at my spine.

"No, I'm okay."

"You should eat something un pequito." She used to call me her "little one" when I was younger but when I got older she started to call me un pequito, which means "a little" I think, or maybe I'm misunderstanding. "Let me get you a hamburger."

Our front lawn is packed with my aunts and uncles and cousins and some of the neighbor's guests—somehow our house is the most crowded on the block, maybe because of the tent. My uncle is manning the grill, prepping burgers and hot dogs to keep the masses from starving while the main courses simmer in the kitchen. There's a table by the stairs set up with wire frames to hold the dishes. They won't be filled for hours.

Auntie hands me the burger and finds another relative to smother so I head into the house past my cousins— some of them officially related and some just friends but we call everyone our cousin for shorthand in my family and this is who I grew up around, at holiday parties and trips to New York state, these cabins by the lake we used to visit every summer. One time all the aunts and uncles who still live in Puerto Rico flew in for a reunion and I got smothered in hugs by strangers speaking Spanish, with intense fragrances covering their faces and plates of pernil popping out of the kitchen at all hours of the evening. I didn't want to sleep, intoxicated by the smells and the tastes and the sounds of celebration, the salsa music blaring. I used to complain about the length of the drive upstate, but I sort of miss those family vacations.

I finish my burger in three hearty bites and move past Nico and a couple cousins watching baseball in the next room. Dad must have picked up fireworks on the way home with Nico because I caught them setting some off at the side of the house and Nico's still dressed in his baseball clothes. I thought about biking over to Stick's to catch him before he went to work, but I didn't want to scare him. I think I already scared him. I'm thinking too much and this is way too tough and I can't believe we haven't talked since the kiss.

"Matty!" Titi shouts from the kitchen, fighting with my mother over the stove, because all their conversations drift into screaming and she gives me a hug around the waist. I smile and move over to greet my grandmother, looking on amused.

"Hi Nana." I hug her gingerly. "How you feeling?"

"Hi sweetie," she says, rocking her slur. She had a stroke last summer and lost all sensation on the left side of her body, but she made it through, she "scared the shit out of death," Uncle Willie said, and she sounds better every time I see her.

"When did you and Poppy get here?"

I'd been hiding out in my parents' bedroom for the past hour, staring out the window in the direction of Stick's house, not that he's home or that his house is close enough to see from my house but I was hoping to use my chakra to spiritually summon him to text, which didn't work, my prowess at ninjutsu is about as advanced as Naruto's in the first weeks of his training under Jiraiya. I may have also watched a mini-marathon of Naruto Shippuden on my parents' television.

"It's two now, Mommy," my mother says. "You got here an hour ago."

Nana blinks and strains to find the clock, across the room by the table where my cousins are fixing sangria. Mom and Titi have quit arguing and are now laughing loudly over the stove, stirrers posed like weapons on the counter, in a row beside the pots.

"You want to taste the rice?" Mom offers.

"Sure," I say, and she shoves a long wooden spoon into the oversized metal pot to grab a chunk with her greasy fingers.

"Eww," I say.

"Relax, I wiped your butt with these hands."

"Oh god, Mom. That's gross." I lean back to avoid her hand and she tries to force it on me, so I jump further away, swatting her arm away, dancing back around the kitchen, and I hear Titi laughing.

"I knew I liked this kid," Titi says as she reaches out to rub my head. I hate when people rub my head, like I'm still a little kid, but I don't mind when Titi Alana does it. She's my favorite.

"And he's so handsome," Nana says. I cringe.

"Yeah, well clearly he gets the looks from our side of the family," Mom says and it's true, or I mean it's true that Mom's side is the attractive one—Titi used to be a model when she was younger—but I don't look anything like the women in my family.

"Does he have a girlfriend?" one of the cousins from the table asks, the Sangria pitchers filling at a slower rate than their glasses. "I bet all the girls at school are after him."

They're not. They're really not. I don't think a single girl has looked at me for half a second since we moved to Woodbridge. Not that I've looked at them either but I'm not tall or remotely muscular and I need braces for my teeth—my mouth is so crowded now that the two front teeth to the right of the middle are growing over each other, beaming out like a lighthouse every time I smile. I try not to smile much.

"He doesn't tell me about girls," Mom says. She keeps her grip on that spoon like a sword but I'm hiding behind Titi.

"He's waiting for the right one, I'm sure," Titi says, trying to save me.

"I wish he would grow his hair out," Mom says, retreating to the stove. "He looked so good with longer hair."

"No. I didn't." I tried to grow out my hair this year, the way Stick lets his hair grow out, but my Puerto Rican curls went into full bloom—what Titi calls the "rainy day fro"— so I shaved it off like it's been since I was thirteen, close and tight with a little peak at the front like a little freak I think, too hideous for the girls in Woodbridge and probably for Stick, he must have been so high he lost his mind when he let me kiss him. When he kissed back.

"Oh crap, the fish," Titi says and pushes my mother out of the way to rip the oven open. Steam comes streaming out.

"What the hell is that?"

My mom reaches out to slap me, but I avoid her again and there's a whole freaking fish lying on a pan by the stove, head on, eye sticking out and staring at me from across the kitchen. I dive behind Nana.

"It's the sea bass," Titi says.

"Nope. Noooooooooo," I say as she spins around with the sizzling pan and steps closer, the fish's purple eye following mine, and its lips—it has freaking lips!—pink and puckered and pressed in my direction.

"See …" Titi says.

"Get that away from me!"

The Sangria women start laughing and Titi steps closer until I'm all the way in the corner behind Nana and she's laughing too. The stench of the sea bass shoots straight through my senses, killing the flavor of the rice and the hope that I might ever enjoy food again.

"Why is that in our kitchen?"

"It's for dinner," Titi says. "It's really good."

"That's it. I'm not eating," I say.

"Oh god, you're so dramatic," Mom says. "It's not that bad."

"Not that bad?" Sangria-ville is cracking up in their chairs. "That's a whole live fish right there. Right there!"

"It's dead!" Titi screams and she can't hold her laughter in.

"Noooooooo."

More roars from everyone, even my mom through her glowering, Nana holding on with her good arm as I duck behind her tiny frame to keep the sea bass away. I hate fish—Mom knows I don't mess with seafood in general and I'm talking about the stuff they serve at restaurants, filleted and breaded and never with the heads attached. There's a whole entire fish with its gross stinking head and its bulging eye following me around the kitchen.

"Stop it!"

The laughter continues but I don't mind, I'm in on the joke this time, and most of the time the women in my family find me hilarious—I mean, who wouldn't, even Stick thinks I'm funny, that has to be the reason he spends so much time with a skinny freak with bad hair and questionable teeth.

"You're being ridiculous," Mom says and heads back to the stove as Titi sets the fish on the counter. I step out behind Nana.

"Sammy?"

"Heyyyyy," he says, kind of slow and dramatic and trying to be cool, or cooler than he is. He said he was coming by, but I forgot in the midst of the sea bass debacle.

"Hi Sammy," Mom says and moves over to embrace him. Puerto Ricans love to hug.

"Hello, Mrs. Tirado."

"You like fish?" Mom asks, reaching for the pan.

"No, stop!" I say. "Sammy's not insane." I grab his shirt to pull him away from the kitchen and all the laughing women down the hall through the party up the stairs, as far from the deadly fish as I can get. Sometimes I think it would be nice to live in a normal family.

※

Sammy's dressed in a white soccer T-shirt and oversized shorts that cover most of his legs, which are really hairy—hairier than any guy I know from school and he's pretty self conscious about it so he doesn't ever wear shorts but it's hot as hell outside so I guess he ditched the jeans.

"Who was that fine Latina in the kitchen?" Sammy's planted on my bed, made nice and neat today because Mom insisted, once she stopped yelling for me to get ready for the party. "The chick with the fish."

"Umm … my aunt?" I say, and I know he means Titi because he's met my mother a million times and everyone else in the room is way old. And ewww.

"Yeah, she's sweet."

"That's sick."

My bedroom is smaller than the one at my old house and I shift the clean clothes Mom laid on my chair to the floor.

She does my laundry but she refuses to put it away so the clothes end up in loose piles around the room, without a home, mixtures of clean and dirty and sort of clean spread out on the carpeting, and the only way I can tell the difference is the sniff test, which isn't the best, but I have no time for home organization.

"Dude, don't tell me you never thought about it."

"She's my aunt!" I say, a little too loud, and I glance out the window to the back. Nico is outside now, running around beside the fence with our cousins.

"Is she single?" Sammy says.

"Get out." I point to the door, but Sammy's sprawled out already, legs spread, the air conditioning blasting because of all the people in the house, and Dad's going to be pissed if it breaks again.

"I'm just messing," Sammy says. "You got my brother's games?"

I squeeze around Sammy's legs to close the door to the bedroom so I can open the closet—it's a tiny room—and I pull out the plastic bag full of Xbox discs Sammy brought over one time and left behind, because his brother had their system down at Rutgers and he couldn't play them.

"Thanks, man," Sammy says. "He's throwing a party tonight and the only way I'm invited is to take him the games."

Sammy doesn't have an accent, not like his parents, but he doesn't speak normal—he's always playing like he's some kind of rap star who gets all the women instead of a skinny Indian who's never had a date.

"Wait—your dad's letting you go to a college party?"

Sammy's playing with his phone, he's always playing on his phone, half the time you can't even talk to him because he's flipping past porn on his screen.

"Ah hell no, he thinks I'm just visiting, like we're going to tour the campus library or something. He got no clue."

The sound of fireworks crack outside my window, out on the lawn next to the house, and I hear children screaming, hyper screaming, Nico by the smoky remains of a firecracker near the fence, where the grass is worn down into dirt. Dad has another one in his hand and lights the flame in the same place, and one of my cousins runs around in a mad circle behind Nico, like she just did thirty-eight hits of Sour Patch Kids and needs her next fix.

"I hope they got weed, though," Sammy says. "I been shy and tripping all week, you know."

I shake my head. Sammy smokes a lot of pot, I mean most of my friends do, but I only smoked once in my life and I couldn't keep it down, I just kept coughing and Trevor kept laughing and Stick held my hand to take the joint away.

"You want to come? My dad's driving me," Sammy says.

Another set of firecrackers explodes in a flood of smoke, and the kids launch into an instant game of tag across the lawn. I glance at my desk, where Kakashi's Story is placeheld by a sock.

"I can't. No way I can leave the party. And Stick's supposed to come by later."

"How is he?" Sammy says. "Is he okay?"

I check my phone again, but there's still no text. I'm not on the phone constantly like Sammy is, or most people are, I mean it's still a lot but Stick's never on social media, so I try to resist and I'm starting to lose my shit that he isn't texting.

"That stinks about his father. Is he home from the hospital?"

"What?"

Sammy doesn't look up, he's just scrolling through screens.

"What do you mean, hospital?"

"Wait—you don't know?" I shake my head as Sammy puts his phone away. "Dude, his father had a heart attack last night. There was an ambulance and everything."

"Are you serious?"

"Yeah my grandfather was out on one of his roundabouts when he saw an ambulance show up. My pops went over and he said they took Mr. Turner to the hospital."

"Oh my god."

I reach for my phone and check the five messages I sent to Stick since the kiss to see if they've been read. They haven't.

"You didn't know?"

"No. I haven't heard anything from him. I thought he was at work."

"Shit. Yeah, it's like really bad maybe."

"Should I call him?"

"I don't know, man," Sammy says. Always helpful.

I let the phone ring on speaker, but it goes right to voice mail and I hear Nico screaming outside the window again, Dad and Uncle Willie by the fence with their drinks, the fiery embers of sparklers smoking on the lawn. I don't know what's happening.

"Where did they take him?"

"JFK? I could see if my dad knows."

Sammy texts and I scroll through Stick's messages, from before we met in the field to watch the fireworks, before the kiss. I feel a brief jolt of relief that what's going on with his dad kept him from texting, not our kiss, and it's wrong, I know it's wrong, but I can't help it.

"He won't reply," Sammy says. "My dad sucks at texting." There's a blast of music from the front of the house, loud booming hip-hop replacing the salsa. "I gotta go anyway, let me ask him."

"Thanks," I say and follow him out of the room.

The tent out front is filled to the brim with grilling and eating and a whole lot of drinking, the hip-hop so loud I can't hear Sammy say goodbye. The neighbors' lawns are as packed as ours now, and several guys are kicking a soccer ball in the street, the Dominican DJ sweating through his shirt as he switches between songs. I fast walk through the side lawn, past the swirls of screaming children, Dad by the fence with Uncle Willie, who tries to say hi and I wouldn't ever ignore him but I'm in a rush and Stick needs my help. I'm desperate.

"Mr. Mateo, get your ass back here!" Willie shouts but I round the corner through the fence, pulling my bike out of the shed. According to the mapping app on my phone, there's a train to Edison that drops you off about three miles from JFK Hospital, so if I can bike to the station then bring it on the train, I can cycle the rest of the way and get there in two hours. Assuming I can take a bike on the train and I have enough cash for a ticket, which I don't, I don't know what I'm thinking, I just need to get my bike from the shed and take it to Stick's, maybe someone there can tell what's happening.

I jerk the bike through the gate, out onto the lawn, pressing hard on the pedals to guide the tires through the grass behind our neighbors' houses.

Stick lives in this huge house further up the street, half a dozen bedrooms for over a dozen children, literally, Stick is one of thirteen kids and he always laughs when I bitch about Nico bothering me, he says he never gets time alone.

I struggle up the hill in the stifling heat and spot their family van pull into the driveway. I pick up the pace on the pedals.

The Turner clan piles out, first Stick's brothers and then a couple sisters then Sherry and Aileen – the oldest – climbing out the front. Stick's the last to emerge, from the back behind Michaela. I don't see his father.

I speed up to a sprint despite the hill, the field to the right where we spent last night in the distance and Stick spots me. He looks up and finds me. I start to smile but he drops his head, shaking it back and forth in an exaggerated motion so I stop, heavy on the brakes, a quick flash of pain shooting into my ankle through the shin.

Stick keeps his head low, following the rest of his family down the driveway toward the house and it's a little too far to be sure, but I think he's crying. I see him crying. I stand on the bike, hands tight on the brakes, as he walks up the path with his arm around Michaela. The pain is overwhelming.

FOUR

THE LAST FUNERAL I ATTENDED was for my grandfather, and I didn't want to go. I mean, I knew I had to and I knew it would be miserable, but I was frightened by the thought of seeing his body in the casket. All I could think of were zombies.

I loved my grandfather—of course I loved him, because you're supposed to love your grandparents and he was nice to me the once or twice a year that they came down to visit or we went up for Christmas, I just didn't want to go to the funeral and I didn't want to see his body, not up close, Grandpop's hollow face brightly decorated around his cheeks and above his eyes, odd layers of makeup over his skin and I didn't know where to begin, where to hold my eyes, so I latched onto the casket to steady myself and tried not to think about zombies.

At the service the priest spoke about a better world, a better place, where we might end up someday if we're good enough or holy enough to hang out with the angels in the clouds and Jesus, I guess, I zoned out for a bit because church bores me mostly and my mind wanders to Naruto eating ramen at his favorite counter serve because that calms me somehow, and church doesn't calm me at all. Not that I hate church. I mean I think I should because the Catholic Church pretty much hates us gays, but I don't mind that much, the new pope seems okay and I like the architecture of the buildings, the dark stained wood along the rafters and the cathedral ceilings, high above us on our hard wooden seats, waiting for the priest to finish. Stick's head is down, on an aisle near the front, his father's body in the casket up on the chancel, like he's on a stage. It's devastating.

They reserved the first eight rows for Stick's family members, his brothers and sisters and older siblings' spouses and children, even his mother is here, dressed in black and sobbing noticeably, but sequestered on the other side, away from the family. We had the viewing first and that was even worse, seeing Stick's father's body up close, the makeup on his face not as extreme as my grandfather but just as unsettling—he's a big man and it's a big casket and when I saw Stick on the receiving line, I hugged him close and felt him cry.

We haven't talked much, which I understand—his father died of a massive heart attack—but it's been hard, not hearing from him, and when we talk it seems like his whole world is ending. I don't know what to say, and Mom says it's good to just be there for him but it's hard to even listen, to watch his face deflate, it feels a piece of me gets ripped apart every time we speak.

I glance over again, across the packed pews between Janice and Michaela, Stick alternating between propping them up and holding on for life. Mom's holding onto my leg and I'm glad that she's here with me but she's been smothering, more than her usual smothering, asking if Stick needs anything and what's happening at their house and whether she should bring over a casserole—like her cooking could possibly help the situation. I'm wearing my gray wool suit, my only suit, too tight in the legs and too short in the arms and inappropriate for summer but Mom said it was fine, she wasn't about buying me a new one. Dad came to the viewing but left before the service and the only good thing to come out of all of this is that I missed a day of baseball camp.

I see Stick's face fall into his hands, and I shouldn't be staring, or I shouldn't keep staring, I don't want him to freak if he happens to notice but I want him to notice. After everything. The priest is going full sermon now, the same repeated verses and the same boring speeches to explain the verses but this is a bigger church than ours in Woodbridge, not that I've attended enough to even remember where ours is located—the last time we went was on Easter and we got there so late there weren't any seats so we had to stand in an alcove just off the entrance, too far to hear what the priest was saying. Like Jesus would have wanted, I'm sure.

Sammy's up front with his grandparents and we were talking at the viewing—I mean it's so shocking, I just saw him, Stick's father, vacuuming the pool at the side of their house. The line for the viewing stretched out the door and wrapped through the parking lot all the way into the street, all the teachers and students who knew someone from the Turner clan showing up to pay their respects. I saw Staci for a brief fleeting moment, but I didn't talk to her and I don't think Stick did either. They dated in the spring, but he said he didn't like her and then we kissed as the fireworks exploded over Woodbridge High. The priest mercifully exits the stage.

The church empties with the family first, from the front, so it's Stick's mom, gasping, led down the aisle by some other old lady and a younger guy—I wonder if that's the guy she left Stick's dad for because she's still with him, and my mom asks about it when she passes—she doesn't know the full story so I just nod and mouth "later." Stick is the second youngest of the thirteen children and most of them are adopted, all the ones closest to his age, but he's the natural born "mistake" that kept the marriage together until his mom cheated on his dad and Stick hasn't forgiven her since.

His face is blocked by the crowd in the aisle, so he doesn't see me as he passes, holding hands with Michaela. I know it's selfish to think about right now, but my mind keeps wandering to the field between our houses and our kiss. And what to say to him now. After everything.

The older siblings are receiving the guests with handshakes and forced smiles and Stick is standing next to Janice and Michaela, out on the sticky asphalt where the hearse is parked. I tell Mom I'll meet her at the car and head straight to him.

"Hey."

His face drops when he sees me. "Hey."

"Hi Mateo," Janice says, pulling me in for a hug, which feels strange, we've never hugged before, but she holds me close, like I want to do with Stick. "Thank you for coming."

Janice is shorter than me, with the same olive skin as my family, her curly black hair tied up behind her head.

"It's good to see you," she says. She rolls her S's in the corners of her mouth when she speaks.

"Thanks. How—" I look over to Stick but his head is low so I turn back to his sister. "How's he holding up?"

"He's able to understand words now," Stick says, almost like he's joking but he doesn't smile. His suit is wrinkled from sitting in the pews and his tie is askew, half unknotted.

"He's still a jerk," Janice says, without edge, slinging an arm through his arm to pull him closer. She's pregnant but not quite showing and Stick is pissed that she's moving out of the house. "He's struggling. We all are."

I nod to acknowledge Stick's brothers—David, Marcus, Anthony, and Jarrett, and say hi to Michaela. Jarrett graduated in the spring and he's going to college up in Maine, but the other brothers are kind of a waste, they sit around getting high all the time and Stick doesn't hang out with them anymore. He says it was different when they were younger, when all of his siblings lived in the house, this big crazy family of multiple races that he spent all his time with.

"I'm sorry," I say. He doesn't respond.

The sun is bright so I need to squint and Stick's hair is slicked down at the side, a style he must save for formal occasions, but the ends are so shaggy that it's sticking up in the back, slick wet with jagged edges trying to break free. Janice thanks some other guests as they move past us. I find Stick's blue eyes.

"I'm really sorry," I say because I don't know what to say and he won't look at me. I feel the sweat on my neck from inside my suit.

"Yeah," he says. No one can hear us.

"I'm here if you need me."

It sounds stupid when I say it out loud—it's like something an adult would say, not me. But I mean it.

"Yeah," he says. His eyes are cloudy like he's been crying. All week maybe. I didn't know Stick's father well, we had like three actual conversations in my life but once I saw Stick at the viewing and as soon as I saw his body—cold and still and deflated, the same size as a human being but flat somehow, like a tire slowly leaking but the air already escaped. I close my eyes and it's all I can see.

"I just mean, you know like—it doesn't matter—" I forget how to speak so I'm just spurting words and I don't know what to do with my hands. I think I should hold him—if it weren't for the kiss I would reach out and touch him, but I don't want to scare him. "No matter what, you know—if you just want to talk or whatever, I'm here."

I've been working out what to say all week, alone with Stick if I could see him like this, to let him know the kiss was just a thing, it doesn't have to mean anything. I memorized some words but I forget them now and it doesn't matter anymore. He grabs hold of my hand.

"Thanks, Matt."

His skin is warm, and his eyes meet my eyes in the bright light outside the church. I feel tears coming on.

"You're welcome." It's a stupid thing to say but I'm out of actual sentences and he's in so much pain I wish we never kissed.

"I better go," I say when he lets go.

"Yeah. I think we have to—" He glances over to the hearse parked along the driveway. Looming.

"Yeah." I nod and he nods and Stick's brothers laugh, loud and unnecessary. I step back.

"Oh, did you hear?" Stick says, reaching out to brush my hand again. "A new World Is song got leaked."

"Wait, really?"

He pulls his hand back but he's looking at me. Finally. I don't even squint at the sun above his head.

"Yeah, someone Tweeted it this morning. Actually, the band did."

"Oh my god, did you listen?"

"Yeah, it's amazing." He pauses and almost smiles and it's nice, to see him smile. "I can send you the link."

"Okay, thanks," I say.

"No problem."

"Maybe we can listen to it this weekend?" I try. I needed to try.

"I'd like that," he says but Janice is pushing on Michaela, who's pushing on Stick, the rest of the siblings climbing into cars lined up behind the hearse out into the street. Stick opens his mouth like he wants to say something else, something profound, but he doesn't speak. His family takes him away.

FIVE

DAD DRIVES ME TO LINDEN for baseball camp every morning, dropping me off on his way to work an hour before practice, and I used to sit in the stands by myself on my phone, scrolling through pictures of boys on Twitter, but lately I've been walking over to Quick Chek to load up on Beef Jerky and Red Bull and Haribo Gummi Bears, the breakfast of champions. We do hitting and fielding drills from eight AM to one, with a lunch that follows then a scrimmage until our parents pick us up—in my case my mom, always the last to arrive, once she gets out of school and through the traffic on Route 1, and we never make it home until late. Stick's been working nights ever since the funeral and when I do get to see him, either Sammy's been with us or Trevor and Gavin are with us, like last Saturday at the Quick Chek by the train station, Trevor and Gavin getting high on bad weed, and Staci showed up for some reason. Stick hasn't been calling as much and I don't know why he's not calling as much but we haven't talked. About anything.

I changed the password on my phone so my parents can't get in, not that I'm looking at boys on Twitter all the time but if Dad found out who I was looking at, even the super skinny dude I watch on YouTube lisping through the different ways to come out and go out (with a guy) and how to decide whether you're a bottom or top (he's such a bottom) and I don't think I can be like that, I don't know how to speak like that and I don't want to dye my hair and get six studs in my nose just to get one stud in my ass, so I'm not sure where I fit in the gay world. And I don't want to come out in my high school—I'm not even sure anyone's out actually, I mean there's some kids where it's obvious but it's mostly girls and I'm mostly assuming because it's not like Sammy or Trevor or Gavin walked me around the halls one day and said "oh yeah, that dude you think is cute—totally gay." Stick's not like that anyway so I guess he isn't gay and maybe that's okay, I don't need us to be gay together, I just need us to be friends again. More than anything.

"Time!"

The umpire sweeps the dirt from the plate and my teammate steps out of the box. We're in the last game of a three-game set against the Dominican kids from Harrison and they've been killing us so far but it's the last day of camp and we're in the last inning of the game and if someone doesn't knock in the runner from first it's over. Finally.

I brought Kakashi's Story to read in the stands before practice this week, I was in the middle of a scene late the night before and I wanted to keep reading but my teammates interrupted with their aggressive existence, ripping the book out of my hand and reading out loud the part where Kakashi drifts into a dream about one of his favorite novels, Icha Icha—the in-universe series of erotic stories written by Jiraiya. They started calling me "Icha Icha" and the nickname stuck, pretty much all week. I haven't made many new friends at camp.

"Strike three!"

My teammate heads back to the dugout and I slap his sticky hand on my way to the plate. The pitcher is new this inning but I think he pitched earlier, the way his delivery is strange and his big lanky frame and I should have been paying attention in the on-deck circle because the first pitch comes out at such a weird angle I don't even think to swing before it's on the plate.

"Strike!"

I can hear my dad screaming, his booming voice ringing out over the cheers from the other team's stands. He's shouting about keeping my eye on the ball and I step out of the box to call for time, sweeping the dirt from the spot underneath me. Dad and I used to watch the Mets and Yankees at our old house, flipping back and forth between innings—he hated the Mets and I hated the Yankees but we used to watch together every summer in the rec room with the air conditioning blasting. It might have been the ankle injury or maybe it happened before, the way I dreaded practice at Woodbridge High, dragging my aching body down to the locker room after a difficult day of classes and more difficult homework and the changing on the benches next to all the bigger boys with their better bodies and their raging … confidence. I was always afraid to look because I didn't want to look and I didn't want anyone to think I was looking so I'd keep my head low and change as quick as I could and I hated going to practice every day.

"Ball one."

The pitcher attempts a pick-off but it's more like a courtesy than anything and my teammate on first gets back without effort. His name is Matt too and he plays for Linden High so he knew most of the guys at camp before this summer. They call me "Matty 2," which sounds a lot like Mateo but is definitely better than "Icha Icha." They haven't let that die all week.

"Foul!" the umpire barks as I take a hard swing and manage to get a piece, but the ball slides harmlessly from the catcher's glove into the dirt behind the plate. Matt steps back to first, head low. I'm the last out of the game.

"Come on Matt, eye on the ball!" my father screams, even louder now, and I dig into the box again, forgetting to check the third base coach for signs. If this were the high school team I'd have to run laps at the next practice but the camp is over today, I don't have to think about baseball or my teammates or my father's constant screaming—like what does that even mean, where the hell else would my eyes be—I just want this camp to be over and summer to be over, so I can get back to school and get back to Stick. Like we used to be.

The pitcher sets up in the stretch and takes a long time to wind up, but I have his delivery figured out, or timed right, I was pretty close on the last one. It's another fastball, I can tell from the spin on the seams, and I stride forward with my left leg, planting hard on my right, the slight uppercut I've perfected at camp driving the ball into play.

I take off for first as the ball clears the second baseman, skidding along the grass into the gap between right and center and picking up speed. I round the base and glance across the diamond at the other Matt, sprinting for third, but my cleats start to slip on the cracked infield dirt and I ease up at once, afraid that my ankle might give, it's just

I'm already committed to second, too far to turn back, and I see the right fielder pick up the ball and release.

I try to speed up again—the cleats sliding left then right but hovering enough just to push off the surface and I'm pretty fast, I've always been fast—but there's only so fast that a runner can go before a throw from the outfield will cut him down at second base. The other Matt is rounding third, heading for home, and if I make it in safe, we'll tie the game. I'm not going to make it.

The ball arrives before I can slide but it's not a great throw—it's too low—and if I slide just right I can avoid the tag and actually survive this. I've been afraid to slide all camp, like really slide when it matters on my bad ankle, so I've tried leading with my knee and my hip to keep my ankle from getting hit but lately, more often, I've gone head first—even though the coaches at camp tell me not to, that I'll get hurt much worse, break a finger or jam a wrist and then it's over, beyond any ankle injury. But this is the moment—no coach would blame me—I need to make this base to tie the game and I can't be cautious and I can't be nervous I just waited too long to decide so I slide too late and I stumble, shoulder first into the shortstop with an unplanned barrel roll that knocks him back off his feet and knocks me clear off the base, flat on my face on the hard cracked infield.

The shortstop finds the ball and tags me on the shoulder and the umpire calls me out. Either from the tag or the illegal slide or for making a massive ass of myself in front of everyone in the stands. I lie on the ground for as long as I can with a sharp pain shooting up from my wrist. There's dirt in my eyes and I can't feel my fingers. I just lost us the game.

※

"What the hell were you thinking?"

We're in the car in the parking lot and Dad isn't facing me, he's got that vein bulging at the corner of his head, by the ear below the temple. I've seen it forever and I'm afraid it's going to pop, in one angry burst of frustration. Sometimes I dream.

"Didn't you know there were two outs? What were you doing on the on-deck circle?" He looks at me through the rearview mirror. "You need to know the goddamn game situation before you step up to the plate."

I've got ice on my wrist from the first aid kit, the blue packs you need to crack when you embarrass yourself with a slide so bad you might have broken your wrist but you don't want to admit it.

"You have to get your goddamn head in the game. You're off in your la-la land dream world all the time, I can see it, I can see it in your eyes. Playing with those stupid cartoons all night."

I've been watching Naruto every night after practice, not the baseball games like we used to, like Nico does now with Dad, but I stopped watching before this summer— why is he just noticing now—and if Stick and me were still hanging out, I'd be spending every night with him, not stuck in my basement watching Japanese anime.

"You ruined your whole day with that stupid play," Dad says, finally looking at the road instead of the rear-view mirror. "Just when I thought you were actually making progress."

My teammates weren't that mad, I mean to them it's only a game and camp is over and they probably won't ever see me again anyway. Someone shouted "typical Icha" and got a rise from the others but I wasn't paying attention, I stuck close to the dugout, receiving treatment on my wrist from one of the assistants. He told me to keep icing it until the swelling went down, to put a wrap on it overnight and keep from moving it too much. He said I should probably see a doctor to make sure it's not broken.

"In what world does it make sense to try to take second there? The play is right in front of you!" Dad speeds through the parking lot to the exit. "It's like you're in another fucking world."

"Jay, stop," Mom says, more than a little late.

"What? He needs to hear this. He needs to learn."

The wrist is swollen and discolored, turning thirty-eight shades of black then blue, from the ice or the instant bruising but it doesn't hurt as much as when I hurt my ankle. I don't think.

"Stupid, stupid, stupid. What did I tell you about game situations, Nico?"

"I think the first base coach was waving him on," he says.

"First of all that wasn't a fucking coach, just a kid on his team."

"Jay!" Mom says. "Language."

Jay don't give a fuck. He's not even looking at her, still focused through the mirror on the backseat.

"You don't even look at the first base coach when the play is to right field. The goddamn ball is right in front of you!"

Nico shrinks into the seat and smacks his ball into his glove, and I give him a glance in appreciation even if his attempt didn't work but he scowls at me because why wouldn't he. Dad's pissed enough to spread his anger around and no one can save me. I hate him.

"I can't believe we sat in those stands for three hours to watch you blow the game for the whole team."

I stare out the window, at the other cars in traffic, trying to concentrate on brake lights and store lights and the wailing sound of an ambulance in the distance but he's already getting to me. I hate that he's getting to me. I cried after a game last year, when I struck out with the bases loaded on a pitch above my head. Dad called me a sissy and said I should keep my head in the game.

"Can't you give him credit for the hit?"

Dad shoots Mom a look like infinite snake blades just escaped from her face, part of the evil ninjutsu of Orochimaru. I feel my phone buzz in my pocket.

"You know how much I paid for this camp?"

Our car pulls into traffic, slow going as usual. We moved to a part of the state with so many malls and restaurants there's a light every few hundred feet so it takes forever to get anywhere. Especially with your parents.

"I told you I didn't want to play," I say, trying to keep my voice from shaking.

"Well you know what, you were right. That bullshit right there showed me I wasted my money."

"That's nice," Mom says. "Real nice."

"I'm not trying to be nice. I should make him get a job and pay me back for this camp."

He slams on the brakes halfway through the next intersection.

"Okay, relax, Jay. That's enough."

"No. They need to learn." The vein is threatening to burst again and I feel excited for a second, like maybe he'll lose control of the car and kill us all in a fiery crash. "Why are you always defending them?"

"Someone has to, you ass," Mom says and I can tell by her tone that she's had enough of his shit today. My phone buzzes again.

"Oh, now whose language are you fucking concerned about?"

"Go to hell."

"Oh I am. I'm going home with you."

They talk like that a lot, maybe more than a lot, ever since I was little or since Nico was little. I think it's been worse since we moved to Woodbridge but it's tough to be sure. I fish out the phone from my pocket, balancing the ice pack on my wrist.

Hey. It's Stick. It's really Stick!

My brothers have people over and I don't want to be here alone. You free?

He sounds desperate. Nico is watching me type so I have to shield the conversation and it's tough to type back with one hand but Mom and Dad are now embroiled in the opening stages of Hate Fight #179 of 2015, if I'm counting right. And I lost count in May.

Yes. I should be home soon.

Dad presses hard on the gas and weaves through traffic without braking.

"Slow down, Jay!"

He slams his foot against the brakes, slamming us all against our seatbelts.

"You're such an ass," Mom says.

Awesome. I would leave but they'll burn down the house without me.

Haha, I say.

Also I stole some of their beer and I may be a little drunk.

Lolol awesome, I say because it's tough to type with one hand and I'm too excited to form actual sentences. The pain in my wrist presses up through my arm.

"Mom, Matty's texting about beer."

"Shut up, loser," I say and reach out to slap him but the spasm from my wrist is so staggering it stops me mid-motion. The ice pack flies across the seat to the floor.

"Mateo Luis, don't speak to your brother like that." Mom turns around to face me. "Jayson, do you see how swollen that is?"

"It's fine," I lie and snatch the pack from beneath Nico's feet, elbowing him hard in the gut. We have a weird age difference—we're not close enough to be into the same stuff, it's like a different generation of shows and video games but we're not far enough apart that I feel some familial instinct to take care of him, I mean I would defend him to the death if he ever got into trouble, real trouble, but he mostly just annoys me.

"Jay, look at his wrist," Mom insists.

"I'm driving," Dad says, veering in between lanes and picking up speed again. Nico tries to slap me back and then Mom climbs fully into the backseat, arms stretched out to separate us.

"I think we should take him to a doctor."

I look up from the phone, trying to assess how far we need to go but it all looks the same, there's too many cars and too much wrist pain, intense enough that I would normally be crying, but I'm too pissed to give Dad the satisfaction.

"What doctor? He's fine."

What time can you get here? Stick texts.

"Like one of those urgent care places, there's one by my school."

"I am not driving down to East Brunswick in this traffic."

I text back with one hand but spell-correct never corrects in the way that you want it to, when you really need it to.

"There's closer ones, you know. What if it's broken?"

"Can you move it?" Dad says, glancing in the rearview as we pass through the intersection. I don't care about the pain and I don't want to see a doctor and I don't want to sit here and stare at my father's fat face. I'm going to go see Stick. Finally.

"It's okay," I say.

"See," my dad says, swerving to avoid a slowing car in our lane. "But there's no way he's going out drinking tonight. He'll be too busy watching baseball. He needs to learn about playing the game instead of watching those stupid cartoons."

"He's not going out to drink either way. He's fifteen."

"Right," Dad says.

I haven't been to Stick's house since his father died and he hasn't come over to mine. There's too much going on even when he's home and he needs to watch out for Michaela. That's what he told me.

Not sure. My parents are on the warpath right now.

"I'll tell you what, I'm having a goddamn drink when we get home," Dad says.

"You and me both," Mom says and for a fleeting moment the tension in the car releases. We speed along a stretch of the highway with no traffic lights and Nico sinks into his seat, away from me.

Just tell your mom you're coming to see me. She likes me, remember.

I lean back and let the ice pack slip off my wrist. The pain is more distant in my brain, almost numb. I stare at the text.

Hahahaha yes, I say.

He remembers the kiss. What we talked about before the kiss. He wants to see me again. It's everything.

SIX

THE SWELLING ON MY WRIST ballooned after the game but Dad took a look and said I'd be fine, in his elite medical opinion. Mom wrapped it up in bandages and Dad started drinking so I snuck out the back to Stick's house, biking one-handed and parking at the side of the garage.

"Who the fuck are you?"

Stick's brother David is a few years older and he doesn't work or go to school, he just hangs out in their garage all day, smoking weed. The door is open like it always is and his flabby frame is squeezed into an overstuffed recliner on one side of the empty space, glass bong on the marble table beside him.

"Ah, I'm just fucking with you, Matt, Stick's upstairs."

"Thanks," I say and make a move to move past him, but he sticks out a leg to stop me.

"You gotta pay the toll," David says, in the protracted drawl he's perfected, too high to speak too fast, at least every time I ever see him. A bunch of his friends are spread out on old furniture on the dusty concrete and the stench of weed is overwhelming.

"Twenty bucks," Marcus says, closer to the stairs to inside. He's the opposite of David physically, dark-skinned and super thin and sporting a thick afro that makes his face look younger, kinder. Stick doesn't get along with him. You can at least reason with David, but Marcus is legit crazy. I spot a guy across the room with a bushy red beard and an elongated face, staggering back and forth on bare feet.

"We're not joking, Matthew," Marcus says.

"That's not my name," I say, defensive over my Latino heritage all of a sudden, or maybe it's all I can think to say. Stick gets into fights with his brothers more often than he can remember—like physical fights, despite the age difference, and his father would break them up and remind them that they're family, the "five brothers," closest in age.

"Well whatever the fuck you want to call yourself, you gotta pay the toll," David says.

"Come on, David, I don't have any money. I just came to see Stick."

My wrist hurts like shit and I've got it hanging at my side, shielding it from Marcus.

"Well you can't pass until you pay," Marcus says. "Them's the rules."

He's spitting on me, not on purpose I don't think, that's just the way he speaks, and the bushy-bearded dude stumbles closer, laughing like he's insane. I try to slip around Marcus to the door.

"Where you going, boy?" Marcus says, hand outstretched against my chest, and I can't deal with this right now, I'm ten seconds from seeing Stick. And I might have a broken wrist. David laughs.

"Gotta pay the toll, got to pay the toll, he comes to the garage and now he gots to pay that toll."

The white dude with the bushy beard starts his rap and everybody laughs, Marcus grabbing onto my shirt to keep his grip as he cackles like a maniac, still spitting, and Bushy-beard is spasming, or maybe dancing, it's tough to tell which.

"Pay the toll, pay the toll, spin around on your face in that stupid sideways place but you got to pay the toll."

I spot Jarrett in the opposite corner by a series of wooden shelves, all 6 foot 5 and two-hundred fifty pounds of him, slumped into a loveseat on his own. He has a football scholarship at the University of Maine so no one messes with him, and he gets along with Stick so I try to get his attention. Marcus squeezes on my shoulder and the pain shoots through to my wrist. Jarrett's playing on his phone.

"Holy shit, Coop!" David shouts.

The bushy-bearded freak slips on his bare feet and takes a headfirst tumble to the concrete. Marcus keeps cackling.

"Marcus, get your skinny ass over here," David says, out of the recliner with a couple random others, trying to roll the passed-out asshole back on his side. Marcus lets me go and I don't wait—I rush up the stairs into the kitchen, away from Stick's brothers and the wafting cloud of bad weed. No wonder he hates them.

※

I remember my first day at Woodbridge High, the jagged anticipation clutching at my chest as the bus looped its way around town, the chatter of the other students drifting past me, strangers staring almost baiting me it seemed, through the massive entrance to the high school, everyone dressed the same but not the same as me, more jeans and less khakis and better hair and straighter teeth. I couldn't find Sammy, who I met in the neighborhood that summer, and I couldn't find Stick, the boy from up the street with the deep tan and the flecks of blonde in his hair oddly iridescent, his eyes inviting and wide like gleaming puddles of sticky blue. So I wandered around the hallways searching for my class while a series of bells rang out in succession and I tried to ask a teacher for help but he was no help—he might have been a student—and I ended up in homeroom ten minutes late. Everyone spun around to gawk at the new kid with the curly brown hair and the Puerto Rican face sneak inside all quiet and shy but our homerooms are assigned by last name, which is so perfect it has to be fate because as soon as I entered I spotted Stick (Turner) and he saw me (Tirado) and there was an open seat to his right on that first day of school. He asked me how I got there, whether I biked the back way across the train tracks. He said no one takes the bus, not even on the coldest days.

"Awesome shirt," Stick says when I enter his room. He tosses me a beer from a cooler in the corner, and I catch it one-handed.

"Thanks," I say, pausing. "What's this song?"

"You don't recognize? Your T-shirt."

He's been drinking, must be for a while now because he's slurring a bit and he doesn't slur when he drinks. Not like this.

"It's their new album!"

It is. Holy crap it is.

"No way. It leaked?"

"Yeah. I've been listening all day for like—I don't know—what time is it?"

He smiles, that sweet unforced smile, like I haven't seen since his father died. He steps across the carpet to close the door behind me.

"Why didn't you tell me?"

"I thought I would surprise you," he says, and I'm trying not to stare but I can't help but stare, a fleeting glimpse of stubble above his chin, the tanned skin and white teeth between pink lips, like right before we kissed. We're alone in his bedroom and I'm nervous being alone with him. I can't help but think…

"It's a concept album or something, all the songs blend into each other and there's this rhythm between them, but I can't figure out the lyrics yet, I mean I've only listened nineteen-and-a-half times—" I laugh, it's so exact. "But it's awesome."

Stick has the album playing from the laptop on his dresser, attached to a single Bluetooth speaker. Twin beds are lined up on each side of the room, one for Stick and one for Jarrett, and I always wondered how the hell Jarrett fits on such a small mattress.

"They're going out on tour. If they come to Jersey, we're seeing them, right?"

"Absolutely," I say, because we need to, definitely, and Stick seems happier tonight, which is nice—we're alone in his bedroom and this song is amazing.

"What happened to your hand?"

Stick leans against his dresser to keep himself upright.

"Baseball," I say. "I think I sprained it."

"That's a massive wrap."

Mom took several tries to get it right but it's not close to right—she's better at teaching than nursing and we probably should have gone to the hospital. But I didn't want to miss being with Stick.

"It doesn't hurt too bad," I lie. He steps closer to get a better look, but he's afraid to touch. The bandages are stacked several inches above the surface.

"You need to drink." He takes my can and releases the tab. I don't like the taste of beer and it doesn't get me high like the glue but I take a sip for Stick. I can't resist.

"Whose beer is it?"

"Some big idiot brought it over, he left it in the kitchen."

Three empties are stacked next to the cooler on the side. Stick stumbles to his bed to take a seat.

"I think I saw him. Big ugly beard, face like a horse."

"Yeah that's him. How did you know?"

Stick waves me over to sit beside him on the rumpled sheets.

"He's passed out in the garage," I say, slipping onto the mattress.

"Nice."

Jarrett's bed is framed by a long machete above his headboard, which I haven't seen before—I mean I knew he was into martial arts, he watches all those Hong Kong action films on Netflix and I get it, I've spent several days at a time escaping to Konohagakure, the Hidden Leaf Village in the Land of Fire where Naruto resides, but it's a little weird to see the weapon unsheathed over Jarrett's bed.

"I miss you, Matt."

I swallow. "You do?"

"Of course."

I left a little space between us—buffer space—and Stick reaches across to tap me on the back, an awkward bro tap, like he's afraid to keep contact. I've been thinking of this moment ever since the kiss, every day it seems if not every second and I feel it between us, hanging between us, this deep perfect something or an unfathomable nothing and I just want to know what he's thinking.

"I miss this, you know. The normal."

He dips his head and I sink into the bed. I was hovering before because I couldn't be sure but now, I think it's okay.

"It just sucks now. I don't even know how to explain it." The World Is swells through the room, sweeping into my head, loud diving guitar into crunchy percussion. "It's like everything is the same as the way it was before but it's not, not really, something's missing—he's missing—and I don't know how to get back to normal."

Stick closes his eyes and the music breaks, slow guitar or maybe violin, I don't enough about music to pick out the instruments, but it's haunting and broken and it's hard to watch Stick hurt like this.

"I told my mom off today," he says. "I was like, you can't come over here and drop off a couple bags of groceries and think we'll be fine with everything she's done—I mean, David and Marcus were thanking her, like seriously?" He opens his eyes with his head low and the stubble sticking to his chin. "I hate her."

"I'm sorry," I say. The World Is fades.

"And I'm really starting to hate them—David and Marcus. They just get high all the time. And Janice is useless, she's never around, and no one's here for Michaela."

"Where is she tonight?"

"At Sherry's."

Stick and Michaela are the only ones underage so officially they're the only ones in his mother's custody, but she doesn't live in the house and she was never around when Stick was growing up so his oldest sisters are looking into taking over joint custody.

"I asked Sherry if I could move in."

He buries his lip in the can and the liquid dribbles onto his chin.

"I just hate living here now with only my brothers and Mom's coming around for some reason. I just can't, Matt. I can't."

He's speaking clearer now and The World Is fills the gaps between his sentences. I take a sip from my can and my wrist starts to sting.

"What did Sherry say?"

"I don't know. I mean, she said she didn't know if there was room for both me and Michaela so they'd have to think about it."

Stick throws down his beer and shakes his head, hard and immediate. I don't think Sherry lives in Woodbridge, and I don't know what would happen if he leaves. To us.

"I'm just glad that you came," he says, tossing his can toward the pile near the cooler and he pulls on my shoulder, pulling me closer. I bought the T-shirt from the band's website—it spells out a play on their name within a black-and-white sketch of an oversized cat. I've worn it so often that the threads are breaking.

"I'm glad I'm here too," I say, turning away because it sounds too gay and I need to shield my eyes from staring, like I want to reach out and kiss him.

"You like the new record?" Stick says, hanging onto my shoulder and not releasing.

"It's perfect," I say. The World is a Beautiful Cat and I Am No Longer Meow Meow Meow. I could stay here forever.

SEVEN

"THAT WAS SAMMY," Stick says, looking up from his phone. "He's almost here."

"Sammy's coming over?"

Stick nods, grabbing another beer from the stash in the fridge and motioning to me. I haven't been drinking—I'm still on my first—but I finish the rest with a stiff forced breath and nod. I thought we'd be alone.

"He asked if we have weed," Stick says, sitting down on the sheets where he sleeps. Next to me.

"I don't have any," I say because he's looking at me and smiling. He knows I don't smoke, or the one time I tried I almost died, and he knows I'm not about getting high in general—except for the glue—and I was going to ask if he wanted to huff because the last time we huffed it ended with a kiss and he hasn't mentioned it since.

The World Is swells a bit and I haven't really been listening but I think this is the moment—before Sammy gets here—where I should bring up the kiss and what's changed ever since because I need to know where we stand. The wrap on my wrist has nearly fallen off, the brown straps hanging down along Stick's sheets. I reach out my hand.

Three sharp raps on the door interrupt all at once and Stick's up off the mattress, opening. A tall girl with thick hair and faded jeans strides past him.

"Umm ... hello?" Stick says.

"Yeah, hi." She moves across to the stolen cooler and helps herself to one of the beers.

"Who are you?"

"I don't know, who are you? Who are any of us really?" She plants herself on Jarrett's bed. "I'm sorry, I've been reading a lot of Sartre lately. And I will freely assume that no one in this room knows who that is."

"What?" Stick says.

"Exactly."

Stick looks at me confused but I'm watching the way his shorts cling to his butt from behind, the way the skin teases the fabric as he shifts back to the bed.

"Wait, who are you?" Stick says but before she can answer Sammy steps through the door with a weird wide grin. It's over. Stick and me. Tonight at least. I take a thick sip of my beer.

"Hey Sammy," Stick says.

"Good, you know him," the girl says, opening the beer and leaning back onto Jarrett's pillow. "I knew he wasn't ISIS."

"Excuse me?"

"Your friend here, they thought he was ISIS." She winces as she swallows.

"Who thought he was ISIS?"

"Marcus and David. They tried to kill me downstairs," Sammy says.

"Are you serious—when?" Stick says.

I glance at the girl as she crosses her legs, the faded jeans super tight against her calves. She catches me looking.

"Just now. They put me in a headlock and said I had to pay a toll to come upstairs."

"That's what they told me too," I say.

"I'll kill them," Stick says, making a move for the door.

"Whoa there, white boy. It's taken care of," the girl says. "I broke it up."

She looks up at the machete, curiously.

"Wait—who are you?"

She laughs, a calm laugh between sips. She seems older than us.

"I'm Cara. Thanks for the beverage. I hate beer but I might have killed myself if I spent another five seconds in that garage without Rhonda."

"You're Rhonda's friend?" Stick says.

"Yeah, she used to be my best friend. But then she dragged me to this party at her boyfriend's house and she left me alone with a bunch of troglodytes smoking weed."

I laugh, this girl is pretty funny, and she catches me looking at her again.

"Where did Jarrett go?" Stick asks.

"No clue," Cara says. "They said they said they were just getting something from the car, but then this kid came in and I don't know, there was way too much drama and who has time for all that."

"Thank you," Sammy says. "You saved my ass."

"No problem, dear," Cara says. "They were high."

"They're always high," Stick says. "You can't even talk to them. My brothers are fucking assholes."

"Your brothers?" she says. "Wait—your brothers are black?"

Sammy laughs. Cara's dark-skinned and pretty and she winces when she drinks. Stick snatches beers for the rest of us and gives her the ten-second synopsis of the family situation—everyone's adopted, he's not, it's weird but it's all he knows, and no one knows what it's like to be one of thirteen children.

"You go to Woodbridge?" Sammy asks Cara.

"Oh god, no. St. Joe's. And after witnessing the level of conversation in the garage, I feel at peace with my parents' decision to push me into religious education. By the way, dear, you probably shouldn't bank on people's general awareness of the difference between Islam and Hinduism, at least not in this town."

"What?" Sammy says.

"Exactly."

Stick laughs and spills some beer and now that the door is open I can hear the party downstairs—louder than when I came up here, with music blasting from the kitchen, Rihanna I think, although I don't know much about pop music. I mean, yeah, I went through a boy band phase when I was twelve but only because they were cute and who the hell knows anything at that age.

"Nice shirt," Cara says.

"Thank you," I say. "I think." Her sarcasm is too thick to tell.

"Yeah, I mean the actual design is pretty stupid—is that a cat?" She shakes her head. "And the lack of style is burning my retinas, but my brother likes that band and he's pretty great so …"

She leans back on Jarrett's bed, against the wall with her beer. Her hair is cut tight around her neck, but her eyes are light and free of the layers of makeup that the girls in my school all wear.

"You want to hear them?" Sticks says, shifting into my shoulder.

"I'm good. I've heard them before," she says.

"But it's their new album, they just leaked it."

"I'll pass," she says, staring at Sammy now, almost daring him to take a seat. I steal another sip of my beer, more than a sip maybe and it doesn't taste too bad, it's slightly metallic but less rancid than before, and I don't remember being this close to empty.

"What's wrong with your wrist, Matt?" Sammy says.

I didn't give Stick all the details because they're way too embarrassing to admit to him and I'm not going to now, in front of a girl—I mean, a woman—I know women don't like being called 'girls' and I don't want to be sexist because I'm very pro-woman, except for the sex part. But that shouldn't count.

"Is it broken?" Cara says.

"I hope not. I don't know."

"Hmm." She shakes her head and finishes the beer. "You might want to get it checked by a doctor… Matt, is it?"

"Oh um… uh, yeah," I say, stammering a little or slurring maybe—have I drunk enough to be slurring?

"And your friends?" She's up off the bed to grab another beer but I'm not sure what she means. I never know what women are thinking.

"I'm Sammy and this is Stick," Sammy says.

"And what are you—freshmen?"

"Sophomores," Sammy says. "About to be."

"Yeah." She rolls her eyes but does it so quick that she disguises it with a smile. "Hang on—did you say Stick?"

Stick nods.

"You mean like a 'stick'?" She holds her hands together with clenched fists, motioning like she's waving a wand, or an imaginary stick.

Sammy laughs. "What is that?"

"I don't know, a 'stick'." She swings her arms now more like a bat than a stick. "It's a weird name."

"Yeah," Stick says. "I was crazy skinny as a kid."

"As opposed to now?"

"Huh?"

"Exactly."

Cara looks to me again and it's weird I think, it's almost like she's into me, the way she keeps looking at me or catching me looking and yeah… no—I must be drunk. Stick leans back along the mattress, this brief electric touching at my shoulder. My wrist is numb.

"Well, here you are."

A taller girl with lighter skin and longer hair than Cara comes crashing into the bedroom. I'm guessing she's Rhonda because Jarrett's trailing behind her, his massive frame filling the doorway.

"Oh, thank god," Cara says.

"What are you doing in here?"

"Bored out of my mind," Cara says.

"Anyone want shots?" Jarrett says, lifting up a bottle of vodka. I watched him play football last fall, Stick and me in the stands at Woodbridge High, and Stick would point out him out during the games, whenever he flattened a defensive lineman who attempted to get past him.

"We need cups," Cara says. "I am not sharing spit with you idiots."

"Okay," Stick says and he's up off his bed, out into the hall and back with a fistful of Dixie cups.

"Fuck yeah!" Sammy shouts and we lift up our shots to do a chug in unison, raspberry vodka that spreads like flames down my throat and I almost choke, it's too much liquid at too quick a pace and I grit my teeth to keep from gagging. Stick pours us another round.

"Damn, that's nasty. What did you buy?" Cara says.

"Stoli," Jarrett says, holding up the bottle again.

"No wonder. That's trash."

Sammy laughs and I wait for the room to settle—I mean it's not spinning yet I just know it's coming quick—as Jarrett pretends to pour the bottle down the back of Cara's shirt. I have no alcohol tolerance, like literally none, a single beer gets me buzzed and hard liquor is like a gaping wound at the side of my head that needs the Yin Healing Wound Destruction to keep me from fainting. I take a second shot.

"Sammy, go get more ice."

"For what?"

Cara pushes Jarrett away and climbs off the bed, ripping the watery baggie off my wrist and tossing it to Sammy. It smacks him in the leg.

"Come on, vite vite," she says and shoos him away.

"My mom's a nurse" is her only explanation as she yanks me off of the bed, down the hall into the bathroom where she doesn't wait, she just rips off the bandages and shoves my wrist into the sink. The water starts to sting but she won't let go, she pushes down harder when I try to pull back, and the frigid water numbs my fingers. My wrist has turned purple, or sort of bluish-black, thirty-eight shades of I should be afraid, and I haven't drunk enough to manage the pain, the way the water keeps stinging.

She finds a first-aid kit in the cabinet above the sink and sprays my palm with clear liquid, which pierces the skin like a syringe or something stronger, a punch to the face. She uses fresh gauze to wrap the wrist once it's dry, across my skin from the thumb down the back of my hand, much tighter than my mother, or much better than she did. She says she wants to study pre-med in college next year, so she's a senior I guess, even though she seems much older. Or cooler.

"Are you okay?" Stick asks when we get back to his bedroom.

"I think so." The wrist hurts like shit but I'm back next to Stick so it's all good. Everything is. "It's mostly just numb."

"That's the numbing spray," Cara says and Rhonda laughs. Jarrett's gone from the room. "But you should really get that checked by a doctor. Like tomorrow."

I don't know why she's taking care of me—maybe she really is flirting but I don't really know flirting and I don't know why she'd be flirting with me. Stick's leg slides against my knee on the bed.

"We need to leave soon," Cara says to Rhonda, looking down at her phone, and I don't know what happened to Sammy. Stick sweeps his hair left to right like he does all the time, and I wish we were alone again, without the girls again, he's drunk and I'm horny and I don't care about my wrist.

"Is that my fucking cooler?"

Rhonda looks up. "Coop?"

The giant freak with the red beard from the garage stands lopsided in the doorway, looking between Stick and me.

"Who the fuck took my cooler?"

He takes two shaky strides across the room to the window and I scan for my beer but I must have lost it or finished it and there's a stack of empties piled up against the wall. Coop staggers toward the bed, red-eyed and wavering. He spots Jarrett's machete.

"Stick!" I shout as the Bushy-bearded lunatic climbs on top of Jarrett's bed. Rhonda jumps up to stop him and I grab Stick by the arm, pulling him out of his bed because we need to escape, and he isn't reacting. There's a drunken giant with an ugly red beard and one hand on Jarrett's machete.

I push Stick ahead of me into the hallway down the stairs and I can feel Coop at my shoulder, breathing down on me, so I'm ducking as we're running, sticking the landing in the kitchen and wheeling around to the left. I stumble a bit as Stick pushes into a crowd of drunks half blocking the path to the garage, so we veer past them through the living room, the sectional upturned and divided to make room for the beer pong, and we plow through empty bottles on our way to the foyer. Coop is still behind us, like right fucking behind me, and I glance back for a second, to check that a swinging sword isn't swinging at my head, catching his stretched-out face stretching out with the machete raised. Stick opens the door to outside.

He decides to skip the steps, leaping straight over the bushes around the porch, pulling on my arm so I follow, catching my foot on a branch halfway through, spilling sprawling on the lawn at the front of the house. The pain shoots up my wrist immediate and quick, but Stick yanks on my arm, yanking me up from the wet hot grass before we launch into a sprint to get away from him, Bushy-beard bounding the normal way down the stairs in bare feet.

Stick spins from the street, angling left toward the woods, this brief stretch of trees that separate his yard from the field beside his house, the one where we kissed on the Fourth of July. I glance back but there's no sign of Coop, just Stick and me through the trees in the dark, escaping.

We keep running until we hit the tracks, deep into the field closer to the trees that surround my development. Stick is breathing hard, I can hear him in the dark, and he collapses to the grass beside me. I follow.

"What the fuck was that?" Stick says.

I shake my head, trying to find my hand, it's too dark to see but I can feel the blood on my fingers, slipping through the gauze onto my wrist. I must have caught it on the bushes and broke the skin.

"No seriously, who the fuck was that guy?" Stick looks at me, struggling to focus. I shake my head.

A car passes down the road into my neighborhood, but we're further from the street than last time, far enough to hide from the headlights. My wrist is throbbing now—this sharp stinging pain from the cut or the sprain, and I'm pretty sure it's broken.

"You're bleeding," Stick says.

"I'm okay," I say. He noticed.

"Let me see." He leans closer, using the flashlight on his iPhone, his elbow brushing into me as I lift up my wrist. It doesn't look as bad in the light but it hurts worse than before. "Does it hurt?"

"Not really. It's still numb." I don't know why I lied

"I should have come over to your house. I just can't be at home with my brothers anymore. I can't."

"What are you going to do?"

"I don't know. I don't know."

He looks behind us for any sign of a machete-wielding redhead, and I hear a train in the distance, like the last time we were here.

"At least we got to hang out," I say. "It's been a while."

"Yeah," he says. "I know."

I wonder if I could kiss him, just reach right out and kiss him. And I know I can't, but I can't think of anything else. The train speeds up along the tracks.

"Everything's such a mess you know. I can't even figure out what to do. And every time I think about my dad, I just—"

He looks into my eyes and I can see his tears forming in the lights of the train, speeding past so fast it breaks his speech if he's speaking because I can't hear him. I just want to hold him.

"I thought I'd be okay. After the funeral I thought I'd be okay." His leg settles on the grass next to mine. "But it hasn't happened, and it isn't going to happen, and I don't know when I'll be okay again."

I reach out to touch, it feels okay to touch—my hand on his back, wet from the sprint in the heat.

"It'll take time, Stick. You just need time." It sounds like something my mother would say—or a fortune cookie—but I'm totally useless in this type of situation when all I can think about is kissing him.

"I just miss him, you know. He'd ask me every day how school went, or this summer how work went, he wanted to know how I was doing at the restaurant. He got me the job, you know—he knew the owner from church so they did him a favor. And it's not like we had these in-depth conversations or anything, but it was every day, we would talk every day, and I miss that. I can't believe how much I miss him."

He lets me hold him.

"I miss this," he says, his voice almost a whisper. "I miss you."

He looks up all of a sudden and I'm too dazed to react, I don't even move when he lurches back, wheeling his head to the right as he vomits all over the grass.

"Fuck," he says as the stench fills the air and stabs at my gut, but I manage to hold it in.

"I think I drank too much."

"Yeah," I say. "Yeah."

He laughs.

"It's okay, Stick," I say, picking him up off the grass and away from the sticky chunks on the field. "You can crash at my house tonight."

He wraps his arms around me, and we stumble forward, slow but steady across the wet smooth grass, through the field where we kissed. I don't want to let go.

EIGHT

I have a theory that waking up in a car
means you're still dreaming.
So if you ever change your mind and
decide that it might be worth the drive.
Then just drive. Then just drive.
So we just drive.
Careless and full of smiles
While the radio plays on the way to some basement.
I will be okay.
I will be okay.
EVERYTHING.

Stick squirts the glue into a rag and folds it into a paper bag before taking a hit, the first hit, always the strongest. The lights are off but the television buzzes in front of us, and I'm still feeling the beer so I feel good, it feels good, in the basement, our basement, this quiet place our personal space, no one else but us. He hands me the bag and I breathe it in deep, letting the spike smack the back of my skin.

We got in through the kitchen, approaching the house from the back as quiet as we could so only my brother could possibly hear us and he wouldn't, nothing short of the apocalypse would wake him from sleeping. Stick is still wasted, even after the puking, and he raided the refrigerator for snacks. We keep the glue hidden back behind the furnace, model cement I used to use for crafting spaceships and rocket ships with Danny Jensen in grammar school, back when Danny lived down the street from me and rode bikes with me and we had a not-so-brief obsession with Dungeons & Dragons and model spacecraft building. He had curly red hair and deep brown freckles that formed intricate patterns on his face. One night in my bedroom, I tried to wrestle with him. He totally freaked and stopped spending time with me.

"What was up with that Cara chick?"

Stick stripped off his shoes and we're sharing the couch in the finished part of the basement, an infomercial playing out in muted scenes on the screen.

"I think she was into you."

"No."

"Yes, she was. She's looking for some Puerto Rican action."

"Stop." I reach out to slap his side and he laughs, we both laugh. This is nice.

"I'm just saying," Stick says, a slick smile sneaking across his lips as he munches on the chips.

"Clearly," I say and touch him again. This is perfect.

No one uses the basement but Stick and me—I forbid Nico from even entering—so we set up speakers from this ancient system we used to have in my old house, tacked onto the wall at random spots around the room. A crazy fat man in a lab coat is singing the praises of a plastic chopping device on the screen.

"Are you gay, Matt?"

"What?"

His eyes meet mine, and I don't know what to say, no one's asked me that before, not so direct.

"I mean, the fireworks night, was that your first—I don't know, 'time' with another guy or ..." He pauses after the air quotes and takes the bag from my hand. "Have you ever kissed a guy before?"

He sucks in another hit, and I flash to the moment in my bedroom with Danny Jensen—a quick stab at touching—and the smile that scared him from the very idea of our friendship. I hadn't been that close to anyone since.

"No. Not before."

He hands me back the bag and our fingers touch, this delicate touching. "Me either," he says.

The man on the screen with the chopping machine shows how fast he can turn ordinary vegetables into salsa, like ten whole seconds quicker than a knife, and I think I feel drunk, or maybe just high. I can't think of what to say.

"Last summer my dad picked up my phone. It was just sitting on the table next to my dinner plate, and he said he needed to call one of my brothers and I was daydreaming or something so I didn't notice. I can't believe I left Tumblr open."

I place the bag on the couch after taking the hit, the images on the screen flickering between highlighting and hiding Stick's face.

"He saw pictures of boys and naked men—I mean, women too, there's a bunch of naked women on my Tumblr feed but way more men than should be on a straight guy's phone." He's quiet, almost whispering, but I can hear him. "So he sat me down and asked if I was gay and I just broke down and cried, I totally denied it. I said I was curious but it didn't mean I was gay or I didn't know what it meant—

it's just that it scared him or something and he started avoiding me for a bit, like even our daily talks stopped all of a sudden."

He stops and shifts back on the couch, and I see his lips begin to quiver.

"But we never talked, you know? I never talked about it to anyone. I thought he'd tell my sisters, or Sherry at least, but she never said anything. So I vowed, like I vowed right then and right there to stop, completely stop looking at dudes and their bodies because that can't be natural—there's no way it's natural—and I didn't want my dad to know me like that, like—he wouldn't understand. So I never did anything—I didn't even look at guys again—not until the night before he died."

I lean closer on instinct but Stick jerks back, the tears about to crack.

"It's just that he was really religious, I mean, it's not that he was homophobic or hateful it's just, I don't know … I'm not sure. I think I was hoping it was a phase, like it would go away when I got older and I'd only want to be with girls, but now … I don't know what to think."

I want to pull him closer, wrap my arms around him, make him forget all the pain slipping down his face.

"He didn't care about that, Stick, you know that. He loved you."

Stick shakes his head. "No."

"Yes. He did. It doesn't matter what you are, he loved you either way." I say it with such certainty like I know it to be true and I think it is, or I want it to be. For me, too.

"So, are you? Gay?" He wipes his face and sweeps his hair and his pink lips are trembling. "I mean, you're my friend no matter what, I just need to know."

Stick blinks a bunch of times in a row but his eyes are clear when he stops. I reach for my leg and pinch at the skin. I want him to know. I want to tell him everything.

"A couple years ago, I was watching ESPN with my dad," I say, "and you remember that college football player that came out—he was like the first pro athlete, or potential pro athlete to come out of the closet and it was such a big deal, like for weeks it was a thing, and all I can remember is when my dad saw the story he said out loud that he 'talks like a faggot'."

Stick nods but his face is clenched. I never told this to anyone before. I never thought I could.

"And my dad's not religious like your father and I don't think he would wish violence on gays or anything but he gets all old school Puerto Rican when it comes to stuff like that—like you got to be a man, a real man, you can't be some gay lisping dude like on TV."

I focus on his lips, not his eyes. They're pink and broken.

"I don't know how to tell him I'm gay."

The colors on the screen spin across Stick's face and he hesitates. I can't gauge a reaction. My legs are shaking and my wrist is throbbing and I think this was a test and I failed, he's sober now and he wanted to know for sure that I'm gay so he can stop hanging out with me. He blinks.

"Do you think he suspects?"

I shake my head. Sharp nails shoot up from my wrist.

"But maybe he does, you know. Maybe all that baseball stuff and making you go to camp is his way of turning you into a man or something. Like all the sports might keep you from being gay."

"I'm not sure spending that much time in a locker room around sweaty boys is the best prevention," I say with a half-hearted laugh.

Stick smiles, the tears now faded into brown smudges on his skin. His eyes are bright in the TV lights, and I reach for the bag for more glue.

"So, you're gay?"

"Yeah." I don't want to lie anymore. I don't even hesitate.

"Okay."

I squish the bag around my mouth to take another hit, long enough to ask him back.

"What about you?"

"I don't know," Stick says. "I don't know what to think anymore."

I set down the glue and reach out with my wrist, the ripped bandage and the dried blood on my skin, bridging the gap between us. "Do you think about me?"

"Sometimes."

"Really?"

He nods. It's not a 'no' but it's not quite a yes and I want a yes right now. I'm ripping out my guts and dropping them on the cushions and the glue is spinning webs through my head. I will be okay.

"Could we try again?" I say. "Kissing?"

Everything.

"Matt, I just—" Stick turns away at first, but he looks back. "How would that even work?"

"What do you mean?"

"I mean, after the kissing, how would that work?"

His legs are shaking, rattling the couch now, and his eyes are clear like he's sober, but I don't know how he's sober. I just want to kiss him.

"Come on, Matt, think about it. We hang out all the time, right? Don't you think it would be weird if we kept making out?"

I shake my head and I almost want to laugh but he's not laughing, and I guess he's right, it is weird. But we nearly got our heads chopped off by a machete-wielding maniac tonight, so I don't know if it matters.

"I guess. But didn't you like it?"

"Yeah, I mean … yeah," he says.

I inch closer on the couch and push the bag to the floor.

"But what if something goes wrong—you know, like that—" MTV must have switched over to Teen Mom because there's a pregnant teen yelling at her baby daddy on the screen. "People in relationships fight all the time. Like my parents. Or yours."

"Yeah but they're straight. It's different in the gay world."

"Oh yeah? You know about the gay world?"

I blush a bit but relax into a smile. "No."

"I'm serious, Matt, if something went wrong and we got in a huge fight over something stupid and I lost you—our friendship." He reaches out to touch my knee. "I can't risk losing you right now. Not with what's going on with my family."

The tears start to seep back into his eyes and maybe he's right, maybe I'm just being selfish about wanting to kiss him, with the way his hair sits lopsided across his face, so perfectly placed. Fuck. Teen Mom is yelling at Teen Dad and I can't process this, any of this, we just came out to each other, fully out to one another, and we need to be kissing. I don't know why we're not kissing. I take his hand into mine. It feels warm against my skin.

"What about a trial?" I say. "A one-week trial."

"A trial for what?"

"We try this for a week, like we really try dating for a single week and if anything happens, if either of us wants to stop or thinks it's too weird then we call it quits, no harm no foul and we go back to being just friends."

He looks at me like he's considering. His hand is tucked into my skin.

"You could do that?"

"Yes. Absolutely."

"No, I'm serious, Matt, if we went out for a week, and then I said let's just be friends, you'd be okay with that?"

"Yeah." I squeeze on his hand so hard that he looks. "I don't want to lose our friendship either. No matter what."

Stick finds my eyes and he sees I'm not lying, I'm way too high to even try and his skin is soft on my skin.

"You really want to do this?" he says.

I nod. And then the most awkward embrace that ever occurred between two people ends with us falling off the couch in a clumsy crash to the floor, wrestling on the ragged carpeting in front of the television.

We grapple for a bit and then we're face to face beneath the screen and then we're kissing, pent-up kissing, mashing lips against lips like deranged sex addicts, and it's perfect. Everything is perfect. His tight smooth body is pressed against my body and it's perfect.

I will be okay. EVERYTHING.

NINE

TONIGHT IS OUR FIRST DATE. Our first official date. I'm kind of excited.

I'M GOING ON A DATE WITH STICK TONIGHT HOLY SHIT.

Yeah, I'm a little excited.

Oh, and I have a broken wrist. The cast runs three-quarters of the way down my forearm to the elbow, extending to the knuckles, but my fingers dangle free.

We went to the doctor on Sunday, after the swelling had ballooned to twice its size overnight, and the official diagnosis is a Colles' fracture of the left wrist. But the prognosis is good—the bone fractured without displacement and the doctor expected a full recovery without surgery. We needed to wait for the swelling to go down before the cast was applied. I'll have it on at least six weeks.

But did I mention the date with Stick? Yeah, you know, no big deal, just a real-live boy-on-boy date, for the first time in my life, and I've only obsessed about Stick since the moment I met him. Ican'tbelievehowmuchthisisamazing.

The only person I'd ever dated was Monica Hopman in the eighth grade, after I found out from her brother in the most unromantic way that "she wanted my body," which I didn't quite get since we were friends and we used to watch Naruto in my living room and joke about how dumb it was that our classmates became obsessed with the opposite sex. Then all of a sudden her brother broke the news that she wanted me, as more than a friend. We went to the spring dance together and I liked having a girlfriend and I liked the way she'd stop by my locker every morning before classes and all her friends would giggle when they passed, I almost didn't mind that she was a girl. But she kept trying to kiss me—this really aggressive kissing, and she always wanted more. She said I never did. We broke up before I moved to Woodbridge, and I haven't heard from her since.

But tonight I have a date with Stick.

I'M GOING ON A DATE WITH STICK!

Did I mention I was excited?

Stick and I talked last night before I went to sleep, a couple hours of pressing conversation, joking and laughter and in-depth exchanges like we're already dating and it's weird—he's right, it is weird, we've spent every day together for the past year but this was different. Better. I had the most amazing dreams.

"What did the doctor say?"

Dad changed into a T-shirt and shorts after work, like he's planning to work on the new shed tonight, and I hope he isn't going to ask me for help. I have a date. I HAVE A DATE WITH STICK! Oh, and a broken wrist.

"It'll be on six to ten weeks, depending on how it heals."

"Are you serious?" He looks to my mom across the kitchen table. "Is he serious?"

"That's what he told us," she says. Mom took me to the doctor while Dad was at work and the casting was pretty painful, this whole week has been an incessant ball of ache since the slide on Saturday but it's not as bad now that the bone is set, and the thirty-eight Motrins I swallowed after the doctor's visit are still in effect.

"And when can you play again?"

He doesn't care about the pain. Or the heavy-ass cast I'll need to drag around the next six weeks. But God forbid I miss any baseball.

"I think he said I could do some exercises like one or two months after the cast is removed."

"You 'think'?" He glares at me, his default setting for his home-from-work state. "What did he say?" he asks my mom.

"That's what he said." Mom's stationed at the stove pan-frying chicken in butter and olive oil, thin-sliced and overcooked. "He might be able to play sports three months from now, I think."

"You 'think' too? Lot of thinking going on at that doctor's office." Dad stands up from the table and moves over to the bar in the corner of the kitchen. "Well there goes the fall season."

I glance at the phone to see if Stick texted. The plan is for his sister Janice to drive us to Menlo Park Mall like she's done before so it won't be strange, it'll be so normal it's boring, just two straight friends seeing the latest Marvel movie and only Stick and I will know we're actually on a date. My dad fills his glass with a long pull from the vodka bottle then a couple cubes of ice, which he lets melt at the table before taking a drink.

"This was already discussed," Mom says, stacking the chicken on paper-towel plates. "We knew it would be a long recovery."

"Yeah, yeah," Dad says, returning to his seat across from me. "Did you look for work today?"

"No." Umm, I was at the doctor's office all day and I don't know where I could work with this cast on my arm anyway and it's not exactly the look I intended for my first date with Stick but okay, be a dick about it. I'm going on a date with Stick. Dad being an asshole isn't going to ruin my mood.

"What are you smiling about?" Dad sets down his drink. I didn't realize I was smiling. "If you're not playing baseball, you're getting a job."

"Fine," I say. I don't have the energy to fight.

"Nico, dinner's ready!" Mom shouts across the house, through the ceiling to his bedroom.

"There's no way you're spending the rest of this summer watching those dumb cartoons in the basement," Dad says. "You'll build that shed yourself if you can't find a job."

"Okay." The summer's only got one month left and he's just being an asshole because I'm happy. I've been texting Stick one-handed all day as we planned out our evening.

"Can you get your brother?" Mom says as she sets a bowl of salad at the center of the table.

"Sure." I've already perfected one-handed texting.

"Who the hell breaks their wrist sliding into second?" Dad says, up and out of his seat to fill his glass again. "The other parents must think you're retarded."

"Jay stop," Mom says, sharp and harsh but it won't stop. It never stops. She does her best when he gets crazy like this, but he hates that she sticks up for us and he hates that we love her more than him. I really do hate him sometimes.

"Why do you always coddle them?" Dad says but Mom doesn't respond, she's back at the stove preparing our plates as Nico tumbles down the stairs to join us.

Mom feeds Dad first, a plate of the chicken with a sweet potato on the side, then Nico and me, fries as a substitute and not as much chicken, I'm too nervous to eat and Nico is twelve, wolfing down the food to get back to his video games.

"So, we have good news for you guys," Mom says, taking a seat at the end of the table while my father jumps up to refill his glass.

"You know how we have to skip vacation this year because of the new house and the move and your braces"— she nods at Nico, still eating at top speed—"and I just got my paycheck for the summer and it wasn't what we were expecting."

We heard this all before, last week at dinner, and I'm still annoyed that Nico's mouth is fucked-up enough to get braces but mine was fine, perfectly fine, even as the tooth to the right of the center pushes on top of its neighbor each day.

"So we're going to pool all our money from this year and save up for the next year and take you guys back to Disney World."

"No way!" Nico shouts.

"Yeah. Way," Mom says and she laughs, that loud cackling cough you can hear down the block. "I think you'll like it even more now that you're older."

"That's so cool," Nico says. He's beaming.

Last time we went Nico was little and no one would ride on the big rides with Dad except me so we spent the day on the toughest roller coasters and the Tower of Terror and avoided the lame rides for the women and children, Dad said, like he was proud of me.

"I knew you'd be excited. How about you, Matt?"

"Yeah," I say. "Awesome." And it will be awesome, although I don't really want to spend a week away from Stick.

"Don't sound so excited," Mom says.

"What?"

"Nothing."

She reaches over and rubs Nico's head and Dad finds the remote for the television.

"When would we go?" Nico asks, half-eaten fries sticking out of his braces. I love the little dude, I really do, but he's so gross it's disgusting.

"Next August, when I'm off school again."

"Can I go on all the rides now?"

"Yeah, you're old enough," Dad says. "You've been old enough. Don't you go on all the rides at Great Adventure?"

We're not too far from Six Flags and we used to go all the time but it's less often now because of baseball and Mom working every summer. She said we could go this month, now that she's done with school and I'm finished with baseball—at least into the fall and maybe longer, the doctor wouldn't even guess when I could grip a bat again. Mom said we should keep that from Dad for now.

The phone rings and Mom gets up to answer. Stick's supposed to text when they're coming over and I'm already ready, or mostly ready, I have my outfit picked out and laid out on my bed I just need to change—I didn't want to get dressed for dinner and arouse suspicion, but I don't want to wear a T-shirt and shorts like every other day because this isn't every day, this is special. This is everything.

"Nico, come here," Mom calls from across the kitchen. "It's your coach."

Dad perks up from his plate, but Nico just stares, like why the hell is the coach calling him?

"Go answer the phone," Dad says, and Nico jumps out of his seat. Mom and Dad listen intently but it's a lot of "yeah"s and "okays"s and I rip through several fries on my plate.

"What did he say? Is it about the travel team?" Dad asks, standing up now.

"Yeah. He says I made it."

"That's my boy," Dad practically screams. "Finally some good news in this house."

He doesn't look at me, he's not that obvious, but I know what he means. Mom gets the rest of the details from the coach and gives Nico a hug and the three of them gather in a semi-circle in the kitchen, away from me.

"When did he say it starts?" Dad asks and my phone buzzes, it's Stick texting so I stop paying attention.

I'm getting ready now. Be over in twenty?

"That's really great, Nico, I'm proud of you," Mom says.

OK. I'll get ready, too.

I'm already showered—which was a bit of an ordeal with the whole wrapping my wrist in a garbage bag to keep the cast from getting wet, but it's been several days and I needed it bad, even Nico was shooting me looks like I stink. But I'm showered and I spent thirty minutes on my hair, testing different looks with different gels and washing them out and combing again which is tough with one hand but I finally settled on parting it to the left, like it always is.

"See what bearing down at practices does," Dad says and I didn't quite catch the rest of the conversation but I'm sure it's an attack on me. Asshole. I made the same travel team in South Brunswick when I was Nico's age.

Awesome, Stick says.

I ignore my dad and his stupid smirking face. I have a date with Stick, and he said it was 'awesome'. I step away from the table and move to the edge of the room.

"Where are you going?" Dad asks, but I don't answer. I just walk away.

TEN

JANICE KNEW SOMETHING was up, either from the way we were dressed or the way we were acting, not casual like usual, but this isn't usual. Stick's dressed in pressed jeans and a button-down shirt and the sweeping poof of his hair is tamped into place by some kind of spray so he looks perfect, better than his usual perfect—is it possible to be better than perfect?—maybe this is a math experiment on the limits of absolutes like something in Calculus but I know nothing about Calculus—you know nothing, Jon Snow!—I just know I'm not making sense, I can't get my mind to focus on anything for more than a second, not with Stick beside me in the movie theater, freshly pressed jeans touching my legs.

"Did it hurt?"

Stick is on my left so the cast is between us, poor planning if I planned to hold his hand like I want to—like anyone would want to. On a date. With Stick. The previews are playing and I'm on a date with Stick. More perfect than perfect.

"It wasn't too bad," I say. "You want to sign it?"

"Sure. Am I the first?" He smiles as the preview for an X-Men film thunders across the screen.

I nod.

"Cool," he says.

I'm wearing a blue polo with flecks of yellow, which matches his shirt, almost like we coordinated so it definitely looks strange and Janice was making cracks for half the ride about how we were dressed and how we were acting, maybe we shouldn't have tried going out in public so soon. Stick covered by saying we were meeting girls—Staci and some random friend they were setting me up with—and Janice bought it, the set up at least. It explained my awkward silence in the backseat.

"I like your shirt," Stick says, and I'm mad that I didn't think of it first, to say it to him, the way the slim folds of his collar blend into his neck, painted on like it's skin.

"Thanks. I like your … hair."

I do, it's slicker and smoother than usual, but I'm not smooth at all and he notices.

"Don't be gay," he says and leans back against his seat, and for a second I'm scared that I've ruined the whole experiment with a single dumb comment about how good his hair looks, like his skin and his face and that smile, oh, that smile. He taps me on the arm above the cast.

"Dick," I say, loud enough to compete with the previews, and he punches me lightly. His knee settles against my leg. More perfect than perfect.

"How was work?" I ask.

"Oh god, the worst."

"What happened?"

"This big guy spilled coffee on himself then he tried to blame it on me. He said I left the cup too close to the edge and when he tried to stand, his stupid gut pushed it onto his coat and that was somehow all my fault."

"No way."

"Yeah, no, we almost came to blows."

"Wow."

Stick's got a lot of fight stories in his family—like way more fight stories than me, and all mine involve Nico because he's Satan's Little Helper, but for Stick, he means real fights, fistfights, where blood gets spilled and furniture gets broken and a trip to the ER is just a Tuesday night. One time several brothers were battling in the basement and David drove Marcus through a wall, like straight through the sheetrock with a hole the size of Marcus's body. The two of them spent the rest of the week repairing and repainting, Marcus with a broken collarbone. They don't stop with yelling like my family does.

"Did you get into trouble?"

"I don't know. He wanted the restaurant to pay for his dry cleaning and I was like, no way buddy, maybe start a diet and replace that tent you call a jacket and forget about the coffee stain."

I laugh, he always makes me laugh, and the date doesn't seem so strange anymore, it's just us. Laughing.

"But my manager's cool," Stick says. "He better not shove me in the back doing dishes tomorrow."

"You have to work tomorrow?" I say.

"Yeah but not until eleven. I can stay out late."

"Good," I say, and it feels okay to say it, we haven't discussed what we're doing later but I assumed we'd hang out in my basement. Alone.

"Are we umm …" Stick hesitates, glancing away from me. "What are we doing after the movie?"

"We could head to my house," I say, under the sound of a preview for a dystopian teen movie. Stick's focused on the screen so I wipe a finger-comb through my hair. "Everyone will be in bed by the time we get back."

"Cool," he says, reaching out to touch my cast, the hard plaster over the wrap now softened, allowing for movement. I'm getting used to it, the weight of it, and he slips his fingers over my free fingers and squeezes gently.

We watch the rest of previews in silence, but this is more than I expected, even in our empty row near the back, holding hands like this. The Menlo Park Mall theatre was transformed a couple years ago into movie restaurants with plush reclining seats and a full menu of food and there's enough of a buffer that no one else is near, this far from the screen.

"This is nice," I say, almost to myself, and I feel him tense up or clutch tighter but I wonder if someday soon, when I get the cast removed, we could actually hold hands in public like this, maybe even in school. I didn't really want to come out in school, but I'd be cool with it if I did it with Stick.

"Dr. Pepper?"

Our waiter-usher interrupts with our drinks and Stick jerks his hand away, quick enough that he might not have noticed if it wasn't so obvious that he jerked his hand away.

"Oh, umm, that's his," I say, stuttering.

The server sets down the drink and sets down my Coke then disappears up the aisle away from us. I don't know what he saw and I don't know if he cares but I don't care what he thinks, or anyone really. I slip my cast over the armrest again but Stick slumps away in his seat, eyes on the screen, the previews ending and the lights dimming and his sudden refusal to make contact with me.

I can't pay attention to the movie, distracted by every movement beside me—is he moving closer, no he isn't, he's pissed at me and my cast is in the way and why the fuck did that waiter have to show up at our seats? And he keeps coming back, interrupting with the appetizer we were supposed to share but it's just sitting there, untouched.

It's obvious now that Stick is freaked – the way he doesn't want to touch me, but then he shifts a little closer at every break in the action or maybe it's me imagining. The waiter drops off the bill when the movie's almost over, but I haven't been following—it's just a bunch of explosions and too much exposition and I couldn't even follow the action at the ending. My cast is beginning to itch, and the food tasted like shit and Stick hiding from me in the dark, not speaking. I let my knee drift into his space, inch by inch before the credits roll up the screen. He shifts away.

"That sucked," Stick says in the lobby, off to the side in the corner by the bar.

I look around before responding but no one is near us. "The date?"

"Really?" He shakes his head and his hair hasn't moved so it still looks perfect.

"The movie?"

"Yes, the movie." Stick swipes left to right, blinking hard in the lobby lights. "The rest was nice."

I breathe again.

Janice calls to tell Stick she's pulling up outside and I dig into my shorts for the pack of mints I brought even though I forgot to use them—I forgot pretty much everything I planned to do because this night has been crazy, it was wonderful and great then it was frightening and strange and I'm on a date with Stick and it should just be great. But I keep getting stuck in my head.

"Did you like the movie?" Stick says when he hangs up.

"Yeah, I mean, I don't know," I say, shifting in my stance. "It was alright."

"Really? What about that whole middle part where they set the trap for the dude working for the government, what was the point of all that?"

"Oh," I say. "That was pretty lame." I have no clue what he's talking about.

"Of course, I'm criticizing a comic book movie so maybe it's me that's crazy."

"Yeah," I say, I don't know what else to say, a crowd from another theater pushes through the doors.

"You calling me crazy?" Stick says and he holds it there, in that space where his smile spills from the edges of his mouth. I need to stop thinking—force my mind to stop thinking—freaking out about everything because he's still my best friend and he's staring at me with those deep blue eyes and that perfect smile. I will be okay.

"Yes. You are legit crazy." His face brightens under the red lights of the exit sign. He loves when I call his bluff. "You should really seek help."

"Are you flirting with me, Matt Tirado?" he whispers.

"Nope," I say, tapping him in the gut with my cast.

"Why not?" He pulls back so I lean closer, up to his ear. "I already got you."

"Oh is that right?" he says, his voice low but not quite a whisper, eyes darting left and right over my head, making sure no one can hear us. "After a single date?"

"Date's not over yet," I say with a quick flirty smile. He laughs and touches my arm at the elbow, sending shivers up my body.

"Good point, my friend, good point."

"Friend?" I say and I let it linger. I didn't think I could do this, I didn't think I could flirt like this. But I am. And I'm not bursting into flames.

"Of course," he says and he shows me his phone, the text from Janice that says she's arrived. "And more."

More perfect than perfect.

ELEVEN

THE TRASH IS WRAPPED up in bags inside green plastic containers, the ones with the holes ripped into the base, and I grab on with one-and-a-half hands to wheel them around to the front. I assumed everyone was sleeping but as soon as she heard the front door open, Mom called down the stairs for me to put out the garbage so I dropped the cans at the curb and hurried back through the backyard into the kitchen, searching for mints because I lost them somewhere and I don't remember where and my breath needs to be as fresh as possible, everything is possible, Stick is in the basement, waiting for me, and my nerves are scraping at the sides of my brain.

I open and close and lock the basement behind me, as silent as I can. Stick is on the couch down the stairs with a devilish grin on his face. THIS IS THE GREATEST MOMENT IN THE HISTORY OF MOMENTS IN THE HISTORY OF THE PLANET.

"Uh so hey," he says.

"Uh so hey to you," I say. He's on one side of the couch and the television is off. He looks as nervous as I am.

"What's going on?" I say.

"Nothing." He reaches around his back, looks past me up the stairs to make sure no one is coming, and sets a liquor bottle on the table in front of him.

"Where'd you get that?"

"Your dad's stash."

"Noooooo, what if he finds out?"

"He won't find out. You know how many bottles he has back there?"

"True," I say, stepping closer to the couch, a mismatched green and gray cushion on one side with the original blue on the other. Nico snuck a stray dog into our old house a couple years back and it ripped all the stuffing out of one side.

"You want a shot?" Stick asks.

I don't think my liver has recovered from the shots last Saturday and I don't know how people drink so much of that stuff. But we made out after we got drunk, so ...

"You have cups?"

"Why, you afraid of my germs?"

"No," I say and Stick smiles, lifting up the bottle and shooting down a massive gulp. It looks like whisky, my dad's first choice of liquor, he drinks it so much I can tell by the smell.

"Shit that's strong," Stick says between coughs. I step past him to take a seat, not too close because I don't want to scare him, but I want to be close to him. I take the bottle and take a sip.

"Oh god."

It's disgusting, worse than the shots from last weekend, just pure foul venom. Stick takes the bottle back for another pull and I know what he's thinking—I could use the liquid courage as much as him, but the taste is fucking terrible.

"You want to play Xbox?" he asks.

"Sure." We've got an old-fashioned fat-back television down here, this massive machine that the movers didn't want to pick up even before they heard we wanted it down the basement, but it's got a pretty big screen and it's decent enough for video games.

"Which game?"

"Crap, I don't even know what I have left, Sammy's brother took back a bunch." I scan the shelf beneath the television stand where the Xbox sits. "Resident Evil?"

Stick laughs. "How romantic."

I feel my cheeks blush at once, but he's smiling as he takes another drink of the whisky.

"Naruto?" I offer.

"Sure," Stick says. "That's vaguely in the realm of romance."

I laugh, the way he always makes me laugh, and find the game at the top of the stack, where it always is. The walls in the basement are lined with gray panels and most of the upper sconces are missing so it's pretty dark except for the television. I sink back into the sofa as the disc loads.

Naruto's video game is not the same as the show—it's got the same characters and the same concept—predestined kid grows into his special powers to become a master ninja and protect his village from various enemies, but it's really just a fighting game, Mortal Kombat-style, and Stick and I have mastered enough attack combinations that we have to keep switching characters to make it even, too many special moves ingrained in our brains.

"Oh, that bitch," Stick says when I pick one of the female characters that he always loses to, but I'm out of practice after all the baseball practice and I'm not sure I can grip the controller with the cast on one wrist.

"Umm…" I hold up the arm and flex my fingers around the handle.

"You'll be fine," Stick says, sucking another sip of the whisky. "Let's go."

The cast is heavy, and I'm afraid to test the wrist so I can't quite thwart his attacks and I get my ass kicked but I don't really care, I just want to kiss him. We play video games all the time.

"Dude, you suck," Stick says and I point to the cast—like hello, this isn't very fair—but he shakes his head and starts another round. "So what happened, really? You never told me."

"Ugh."

"Mateo Tirado."

He never calls me that, but I like when he calls me that. His eyes are red and mine are blurry and Naruto's music plays low in the room.

"I tried to slide, you know, without sliding on my ankle and—" He's laughing already and I don't want to finish, I just want to kiss him, but he's not making fun of me. He never does. "So I did this sort of unplanned barrel roll and slammed into the dude at second base and I busted my wrist and they called me out anyway."

"Oh my god," Stick says, bent over clutching his chest from all the laughter. I reach for another drink, I don't care about the taste.

"Oh my god, that's so great."

"Nope," I say, wincing.

"What did your dad say?"

"That I'm a goddamn spaz."

"Of course," Stick says.

I set down the bottle and I'm waiting, I keep waiting, I figured Stick would make the first move once we got to the basement, he's the more adventurous of the two of us usually, like at Six Flags this spring we were on a class trip and the rain shut down all the rides so when the sun came out, Stick convinced the operator to let us on Nitro even though the tracks were wet. The cars bounced off the rails the entire ride and I'm pretty sure we could have died. But he's acting all casual now like we're just friends hanging out and maybe that's okay, because this needs to be normal and he needs to be okay with this but I really want to kiss him. Stick turns to me and I don't want to wait.

"I like your shirt," I say.

"I told you not to be gay," he says with a quick slick smile and I can't resist, I inch forward on the mismatched cushions. He glances behind him, up the stairs.

"Don't worry, I made sure it was locked," I say.

"Okay," Stick says and grabs one last drink from the bottle, setting it on the table beside us. And before he turns I've already lunged across the space between us, eyes open to guide my lips to his lips, swift and intense and holy shit, THIS IS HAPPENING! I shift closer, my still eyes open—am I supposed to close them?—then I'm on top of him, fully on top of him, and we're kissing.

Stick pulls back and his eyes are rolling up in his head like he can't control them, then he pushes me back, against my back, my legs scrunched up to my knees until they almost don't bend anymore. He leans into me, on top of my chest, pinning my arms against the cushions as he reaches under my shirt, touching.

I try to catch my breath but I start shaking, I can't stop shaking. I can't actually breathe and I can't stop shaking. This is amazing.

"Here," Stick says, reaching out for my polo, pulling it up to my chest and I do the rest, yanking the shirt over my head and out one arm but it gets stuck on the cast so I can't remove it without him helping but he's too busy touching and then we're laughing, this brief burst of laughter like "holy shit, what is happening?"—and then we're kissing again, rubbing and touching on our backs and bare skin, his lips on my lips, my shirt on my wrist.

He retreats for a second to unbutton his shirt and I take the lead again, pushing forward into him. I close my eyes and it's better this time. So much better.

I let my right hand explore, above his waist but along his back and his side, pausing at the stomach, this little bulge above his hips, and his hands drift down along my chest—past the stomach to my waist, my cast in the way but we're not waiting, it's just happening. I CAN'T BELIEVE THIS IS HAPPENING.

"Oh my god!"

My mom's voice is unmistakable in any situation, especially in this situation, three steps from the bottom of the stairs.

Stick jumps up first, attempting to button his shirt and zipping up his jeans.

"What in the hell is going on down here?"

Stick looks at me, eyes darting all over my face, but I don't move, startled and shaken and frozen in place.

"Nothing, Mom, nothing," I say, but it's too late, she's standing in the basement and Stick is backing up against the television, away from me.

She's dressed in her oversized sweats and glasses and she can't keep her eyes from switching back and forth between Stick and me. I thought I locked the door—I know I locked the door, how the hell did she get down here?

"Wow, umm, wow," she says, lower now. She turns her focus to me not Stick but I'm stuck to the ragged cushions, unable to push off with my broken wrist to get dressed again, or move again, or do something other than sit and stare and hope for the world to end.

"You should probably go home, Stick," Mom says. He's already near the stairs, stepping around her, shirt buttoned now and hanging over his jeans. "I need to talk to Mateo."

"Okay," Stick says, and he doesn't hesitate, he's up on the bottom step, looking back at me for half a second before sprinting up the stairs out of the basement. I want to call out—I try to call out, but I forget how to speak or I can't hear myself speak, the piercing ringing in my head shattering the bones of my middle ear—the smallest bones in the body, according to my biology teacher, which—why the hell am I thinking that now?

"What have you—how long have you—are you and Stick?"

My wrist is throbbing, this deep stinging ache, and a pressing rage replaces the shock in my brain.

"How did you get in here?"

She looks at me lopsided because she can't see without her contacts and Naruto is running an endless loop on the screen.

"Are you gay, Mateo?" Her words spill out at such a high pitch that all the dogs in the neighborhood begin to bark in unison and the tiny bones of my middle ear implode and break. I need to blink to breathe. I can't breathe.

"What? No."

She laughs—she actually fucking laughs. "Are you sure?"

She's staring me down like I'm this alien creature she discovered in the basement and she doesn't know whether to yell or to scream. I can't believe Stick is gone—I'm pretty sure I was seconds away from whatever base it's called where I could touch his dick. I don't know what the hell is happening.

"Matty," she says, stepping closer to me on the couch. "You can talk to me."

I've never really thought about the moment of my coming out—like the actual moment, what I would say and how I would say it, I mean I definitely never imagined it would be in my basement with a shirt hanging off my wrist and Mom squinting at me like this. I wanted to be prepared, more prepared, I mean yeah, I've always known I liked boys, but I never prepared for this.

"Matt." She reaches for my elbow but I pull back. I don't want her to know. I don't want anyone to know. Not yet.

"It's okay. There's nothing to be ashamed about." She knows she's lying but she doesn't want me to freak. "We can talk about it, sweetie, you don't have to be embarrassed or anything. We don't have to tell your father."

"Do not tell Dad!" I say, jumping off the couch. "I'm not gay and you saw nothing, okay?"

I shoot her the angriest glare I've ever given anyone in my life but she's immune to my anger. And I'm not actually wearing a shirt.

"Matty, calm down, let's just talk," she says.

"There's nothing to talk about." I push past her toward the stairs, my shirt at the end of my cast. "Nothing happened and you didn't see anything and I'm going to bed."

She waits without speaking and I know she wants to get it all out of me, how fucking gay I am and how many boys I've kissed and I should really use protection because of HIV and STDs and I can't think of that now, I can't think of anything except how she ruined it—she ruined everything. I think for a second I should chase after him, try to catch him, but I'm not sure how long we were down there without him and I don't know where he went. I hear Mom follow me through the kitchen.

I rush up the steps two steps at a time, down the hallway into my bedroom, locking the door three times and sticking my chair against the handle. I text Stick one-handed and bury my head in headphones, to drown out the sound of her existence.

He doesn't text back, and I can't help it, I can't stop them. The tears break the surface. I'm out to my mom and I didn't want to be out, not like this. Not without Stick.

Kakashi's Story is on the desk in front of me and I let my face smack the cover when I collapse, headfirst to the surface. Mom knows and now Dad's going to know and Stick was already freaking before this. Mom knocks at the door and I can tell that she wants me to open it but I'm not going to speak to her. Ever.

Stick may never speak to me again.

TWELVE

"HEY MATTY!" Janice sees me first, along the road to my development, and I pick up my pace on the pedals. Stick hasn't texted and I tried to wait but I couldn't keep waiting, thirty-eight thousand Naruto marathons not enough distraction to keep me from freaking, full-on panic every second it seems, and I rushed down the street when I saw him bike home from work. The words come out in a rush.

"Where you guys going?"

"The cemetery," Stick says.

"We're going to see Dad," Janice says, searching through her purse for the keys. "We haven't been since the funeral."

I nod and look to Stick but his head is down. Lifeless. It's been three days.

"What happened to your arm?" Janice says with the keys dangling.

"Baseball. Broken wrist."

"Oh wow. Does it hurt?"

"Not really." And it doesn't, not really. It just itches.

"Did you need something?" Janice asks, clicking open the doors. The awkward is in the air, the ghostly remains of our former friendship.

"Just came to see Stick," I say, in an appropriate third person since he's not speaking to me, or even looking at me, three full days since the fated end of it, in my basement on the mismatched cushions, and I can't get it out of my head.

"Sorry, man, not a good time," Stick says, opening the passenger side. He's wearing his bus boy uniform—white shirt and black bow tie loose around his neck, smatters of grease along the leg of his pants. He always works the lunch shift on Saturdays so I've been watching down the street, waiting for him all day. He climbs into the car without waiting.

"Do you want to come with?" Janice asks. Stick's not bothering to hide the tension and she can sense it.

"That's alright," I say. "It's a family thing."

"You know you're family, Matt. You're more than welcome to join."

Stick's door is open, but he doesn't want me to come, he doesn't want to see me after Mom ruined everything and I get it—I'm pissed at her too. But that doesn't make it hurt any less. I nod and climb into the back seat.

Janice does most of the talking on the ride to the cemetery, about her apartment search and her morning sickness—vivid descriptions of the volume and the color of the chunks spewing from her gut—and no one is protesting because no one is speaking, we're just listening to the stereo but nothing's on, there's never anything good on, so Stick keeps switching stations and ignoring me completely, the entire way through the black iron gates into the cemetery.

"Do you remember which way it is?" Janice asks. She glances at Stick, but he doesn't say, he hasn't turned his head away from the street. He hates me.

"I think it's this way," she says to herself and turns down a dirt road a few hundred feet past the entrance. The head-stones are low and shrouded by tall weeds and Stick turns off the radio so we sit in silence as we ride, the trees partly green but covered with patches of brown that make it look dark even in the daytime, this boundless gray suffocating the light. I don't know how I feel about an afterlife, like I don't believe in ghosts and stuff like that—zombies yes, but only in fiction, I just wonder what happens when you die, to your body I mean—how far down it goes and how long it takes to decompose, how many years before the wear of the soil cuts through the wood and the bugs bore into your bones.

"We should have brought flowers," Janice says, swinging left into a newer part of the cemetery, the road paved with stones and the lawns freshly mown. "Every site has flowers."

We drive through a mass of trees to a dead end it seems, even darker now, the oversized houses of some new development separated from the cemetery by a high white fence. Janice's car is sputtering, and the air conditioner isn't reaching the back anymore, so I shift in my seat, struggling to breathe.

"Which way do you think?" Janice says, looking over to Stick but he doesn't respond. "You know, you're really being helpful today."

He still hasn't spoken. Even Janice noticed. Finally.

"Sorry," Stick says. "I think it's over there."

She pushes the car into park and shuts off the engine. "You okay?"

"No," Stick says.

I tense up, sinking down in my seat.

"Mom?"

"Yeah," Stick says. "What the hell is she thinking?"

Janice reaches over to take his hand and I know they're pretty close—Stick told me that when Sherry moved out, Janice took care of him, because his mom never really mothered them, and I kind of wish I had a sister, or an older sibling, someone who understands the anger I feel for my parents in a way Nico can't.

"Our lovely mother showed up this morning with her boyfriend," Janice says through the rearview mirror. "She might be moving back in."

"Really? She can do that?"

"Yeah. The house is still in her name and she's fighting Sherry and Aileen for custody of Michaela. And Stick."

"Oh."

"Yeah, it's bullshit," Stick says. "It's all for show, you know it's all for show. She doesn't give a shit about me."

"I know," Janice says.

"Don't say 'you know'—you're not even going to be there," he snaps. "You're leaving."

"You know I have to move out," Janice says, touching her stomach. "I said you could move in with us."

"To some tiny apartment with your loser boyfriend?"

"He's not a loser."

Stick rolls his eyes. "I'm just saying."

"You can watch the baby," Janice says, and she laughs when she sees Stick's reaction—if there's one thing Stick and me have in common it's that we're not about children. Especially babies.

"Do you think Mom's boyfriend is moving in too?"

"Probably."

"Fuck that shit," Stick says. "I can't. You know I'm going to tell him to get the fuck out on day one."

Janice laughs but Stick's not laughing and the sun peeks through the leaves into the front seat between them.

"I'm serious. How the hell can she cheat on Dad and then bring him into our house?"

"Yeah," Janice says, reaching out again but she can't calm him, nothing's going to calm him. I can't stand my mother for what happened in the basement, but at least she didn't break up our family. I have no frame of reference.

"And David and Marcus were all smiley with her, laughing and joking like nothing happened."

"They just want to live there without paying rent," Janice says.

"Yeah." Stick drops his head. "But it's not the same. You're moving out and Jarrett's leaving for school and Michaela's never around. I can't live in a house with just David and Marcus and Mom, of all people."

He trails off and faces the window. It's hot in the car with the engine off. I try the window by my side but it doesn't go down.

"What did Sherry say about moving in with her?" I ask.

"I don't know," Stick says. "She hasn't said."

"I don't think there's room right now with Michaela there," Janice says. "What about Aileen?"

"I'm not living with Aileen. She's like a drill sergeant. And she lives way the hell out in PA."

"Yeah," Janice says. "Well, maybe Mom won't end up moving back."

She reaches out to Stick again but he retreats to the corner of his seat, cheek flush against the window. His mom left before I met him, but he hasn't forgiven her and he says he never will. So, I guess this isn't about me. Not completely.

"You can stay with us," I say.

The silence spreads through the vehicle, this sudden silence in the whole of the graveyard. The gravesites rise around me.

"I mean, if there's nowhere else. You wouldn't have to change schools."

I shift in my seat and he still doesn't speak, but I didn't mean anything by it, I really didn't. I just want to be there for him.

"See, there you go," Janice says. "We'll figure something out."

"I'm sure your mom wouldn't be opposed to that for any reason," Stick says, turning halfway, and it stabs me in the gut—the way his eyes shoot out of his skin with his anger over everything.

"Come on, let's go see Dad," Janice says, and Stick jumps out of the car behind her. All I can do is follow.

The gravesite isn't far from the road, halfway up a hill, and their father's headstone is the standard straight-up marble kind, but most of the others are lower, tucked into the ground, so you can almost spot his from the street, if you know where you're looking. It's a simple engraving cut into the stone, his name and the dates and "Beloved Father and Grandfather" in cursive text. No mention of a wife.

"Come on, Matt, you can come closer," Janice calls, waving me forward. They're arm in arm at the headstone and the sun is bright, the trees around this site less covered with leaves. I step over the dirt in my Vans and board shorts, not exactly dressed for the occasion but then Stick and Janice aren't dressed up either. Maybe cemetery visits are come as you are.

"You know Dad didn't like too many people who came over—like with David and Marcus, their friends are degenerates, so Dad would openly moan when anyone showed." She laughs and wraps her other arm around me, pulling me closer. "But he liked you. He even told me one time that he was glad Stick was hanging out with a 'good kid,' not the idiots Marcus brings home."

She smiles and I look past her to Stick, and I think he might be crying, the way the blurred streaks trail along his cheeks.

"Shit," Janice says, pulling out her ringing phone. "It's work."

She walks off to take the call and Stick steps closer.

"What did your mom say?"

The tears are still wet on his skin, deeply tan like it's been since the start of the summer.

"Nothing."

"Don't play dumb, Matt, what did she say?"

"I told you she hasn't said anything. She tried to talk to me, but I wouldn't let her. I denied everything."

"Denied what?" He glances behind him to make sure Janice isn't listening but she's halfway down the hill with the phone in her hand. "She saw us, didn't she?"

He moves on top of me, almost into me, and my mind is swimming with all these propositions about how nothing needs to change, we can make it all the same, like before Mom came into the basement. She doesn't even care—I mean she cares but I can put her off and we can be more careful about where we do things together and go back to the experiment with the dating because it was working— he knows it was working. We could start again.

"She doesn't know what she saw, and I told her it never happened before, and she promised she wouldn't say anything."

"Did she ask about me?"

"No," I say, and that part is true. All of it is true. I need him to believe me.

He turns to the headstone, the words big and bright in the sunlight. "I wasn't here when they laid the stone."

"No?"

He steps back one step. Closer to me.

"Yeah, I was working, and I tried to take off but it was too late and my sisters didn't tell me. Apparently, I'm too young to be a part of the decisions that affect my life." He sniffs. "I mean, even when Dad went to the hospital and I was with you, they could have called, I had my phone on, but no one thought to call me. They never think about me."

I reach out but he shakes me off, his head still low, and I want to put my arms around him, take all that pain and put it on me. I love him. He needs to know.

I try again to take hold of his fingers. He lets me.

Janice returns and says she's got to go to work and Stick asks to be alone for a moment. By the stone.

"Okay," she says and gives her father a weird giggling goodbye before retreating to the car in a rush. Stick speaks to his father with his lips moving but no words coming out and his fingers are tight around my thumb.

"I miss him so much," Stick says, out loud, the tears flowing again.

"I know," I say and extend an arm around his back. It's quick and he resists but then he lets me. I don't want to let go.

THIRTEEN

"STRIKE ONE!"

"Good pitch, Nico, good pitch!"

Nico's on the mound in the second game of possibly three, a long, long night on the hot metal stands with the heat seeping through my shorts into the skin, melting my legs into puddles of sweat dripping onto the grass but I don't mind, I don't even notice the pain, I'm too focused on Kakashi trying to prevent the Tobishachimaru from floating too high and taking all their lives, or worse, getting shot down from below on orders from Lady Tsunade.

"Take your time, Nico, don't rush the pitch!"

Dad is barking out orders at the top of the stands, teetering on the edge of my row, and he might collapse if that vein explodes, like the ballast on the airship, shattered in an attack between the clouds, and the Tobishachimaru keeps rising, thirteen thousand meters above the ground.

"Ball three!"

"Come on, Nico, take your time."

Nico's team won the first game, and he's pitched well in the second so this night might mercifully end if he doesn't

give up any runs this inning but he must be struggling—
Dad's been on his feet for a while now.

"Ball four."

I look up from my book and see the bases are loaded,
Nico pacing around the mound as his coach comes out for
a visit. Dad takes a seat, but the bulging vein is blue and he
looks over at me like he's about to yell so I jerk my head
back to the story. Kakashi flings his chakra-infused kunai
into the helium-filled bladder, piercing the skin with the
blade and sending the airship tumbling, a last desperate
chance to stop its rise.

"All right, come on Nico, take your time, bear down
and get this guy," Dad says, less shouty this time, but he's
already driven away all the fans from our side of the stands,
huddled in a frightened mass at the other end. Mom and
Titi are down on the grass in the beach chairs they brought
from the car—"No way I'm burning my ass on that metal,"
Mom said, and my nieces are running around at the edge
of the field, losing their minds in the heat.

"Ball two!"

Nico wipes his mouth with the back of his wrist and his
face gets smeared with mud. It's rained all week, ever since
the cemetery visit, which seems appropriate. I thought we
were okay, or I thought we'd be okay, and even on the ride
home Stick laughed when Janice asked if I was seeing the
girl Staci "set me up with," but his texts have been super
short and it's been really long between responses and it's
getting kind of sick to think of him like this, like we're no
longer best of friends.

"Can you pay attention to the goddamn game," Dad
shouts, glaring at me from the top of the stands and at
first I don't get that he's talking to me because he hasn't

talked to me all night. "You're at a baseball game and your brother's on the mound and you're sitting there reading— what is that, one of those cartoon books?"

"It's a real book," I say, defensive for some reason, and it's true—it's a novelization of an episode of Naruto Shippuden, not manga, not that it should matter, I shouldn't have to defend myself to him. He never reads. "Mom bought it for me."

"Figures," he says, shaking his head and teetering further near the edge of the row again and I almost want him to fall, tumble to the earth like the Tobishachimaru—break his own wrist in the process. "What, did you give up on baseball for those stupid comics? Pathetic."

He's loud enough that the rest of the stands can hear us, unless they tuned him out already, which maybe they have because he's like this all the time, his way of "cheering" for Nico and me.

"Strike!"

"That a boy, Nico!"

Dad claps loudly and I don't know the count or how many outs but I don't really care—I've been here too long and the Tobishachimaru is now plummeting to Earth! Kahyo's mission has failed but she joins Kakashi's side and uses her jutsu to throw a chakra-cloaked ice slab underneath the airship, hoping to slow its fall.

"Smack!"

The ball explodes off the bat, a long shot deep into center, and Nico's teammate races back, spinning around as the fence approaches, this tiny 11-year-old chasing the ball like the fate of the tourists aboard the Tobishachimaru depend upon this moment. He reaches out to make the catch and slams into the fence at full speed.

"Holy shit!" I shout, not even aware as the words leave my mouth and the kid is sprawled out on the grass. The runners tag up then start to race around the bases and Nico's coach and a couple teammates rush into the outfield, the centerfielder not moving. Dad steps down the stands.

The Tobishachimaru is falling, not as fast as it was, but there's not enough water in the air for Kahyo's jutsu to build enough ice, so the slab keeps melting and the ship keeps dropping in altitude. Kakashi orders Kahyo to continue weaving signs as he focuses every chakra in his body into his right arm, pointing up at the clouds with a lightning bolt to make it rain. Literally.

"Hey kid."

I look up from the book and spot Nico's teammate getting helped off the field.

"Hi Titi."

"How you doing?" She climbs up to me with her pregnant belly extended and reaches out for a hug. I can smell the shampoo in her hair, like lavender. "How's the wrist?"

"Getting better, I hope," I say, setting the book aside. The coaches and umpires are meeting in a semi-circle near the mound and Dad presses his body against the fence.

"Let me see." Titi reaches for the cast, gingerly, but it doesn't hurt to touch. "You want me to sign it?"

"Sure." She fishes for a pen in her purse.

Stick signed it after the movie, just his name, just "STICK," and I have other messages like "All the best" or "Get well" or "Try Not to Trip Again" (freaking Nico), but Stick's name is in big red letters on the inside, close to me.

"How's your book?"

"It's good," I say. The game is paused and it's getting dark all of a sudden and my cast is itching from the heat.

"Is that Naruto?"

"Yeah," I say. It's not really, it's Kakashi, Naruto's sensei, and it's like a one-off adventure that turned out to be a really good story and I'm right at the ending but it's a little embarrassing to tell all that to Titi, no way she cares about Kakashi's mission to the Land of Waves to rescue hostages from a top-secret airship.

"Which one is it?" she asks. The coaches have moved around Nico on the mound.

"It's about Kakashi," I say, "Naruto's team leader so it's different from the stories in the show. Mom bought it for my birthday. I don't think she knew what to get."

Titi laughs. "I never know what to get you either. Hence the gift cards. Of course, if I did know what went on inside the mind of a fifteen-year-old boy that would be a little disturbing."

She laughs again and it's nice for a moment, she always finds a way to calm me. There's a runner at third and the inning's still going on I guess—I think this game might be part of an experiment to test whether skin on metal can legitimately melt in this heat. The coach replaces Nico with another pitcher.

"So what are you doing tomorrow?" she says.

I shake my head. "Nothing."

"You want to do a Titi and Matty day?"

"Really?"

"Yeah, sure. You said you were free, right?"

We used to have Titi and Matty days all the time when I was little, after Nico was born. I'd get dropped off at her apartment and we'd make popcorn for Disney movies—she still loves Disney movies—and she got me hooked on staying up late and quoting lines from all the classics.

"What about the girls?"

"Your mom said she'd watch them for me."

"Really?"

She nods and I glance back at the field. Dad's crossed the fence to the edge of the dugout, yelling at the coach, I think.

"What do you want to do?"

"I thought we could go to the mall—your mom says you refuse to go clothes shopping for school." I scrunch up my face—I hate clothes shopping—and Titi laughs. "Or not."

"I mean, the mall's okay but could we see a movie, too?"

"Sure." She reaches across the bench and touches my knee. "I don't know if there are any Disney movies out, but we could check."

"Great," I say and I hear my dad screaming, at the coach in front of him, screaming back. "Titi?"

"Yeah, sweetie?" She turns back, half distracted by Dad's anger that Nico got pulled from the game. He pushes the coach in the chest.

"Did Mom say something to you?"

"About what?" She turns back too quick and now I'm convinced that she knows about Stick and me. She definitely knows. I weave a withering glare in my mom's direction but she's over by the fence yelling, too.

"Nothing," I say.

Mom's horrible with secrets but she didn't tell Dad because he's still being a dick to me, in the usual way, and I know he would act different if he knew, the way everything is different now and I don't want to admit it. Mom tried to talk to me the day after, about what she saw or she thought she saw, plopping down on my bed with her pressed solemn face, spinning this long pointless story about her best friend in college who hid his "sexuality" from her—she actually used that word, on my bed next to me, and that's when my eardrums exploded and my face burned to ash, and I couldn't hear anything else she said.

"Are you okay?" Titi says, stepping back with blinking eyes and rubbing my head. I love her to death, but I don't want her to know. Not yet. It's not that I want to keep it a secret forever, but I haven't had the time to process it yet and I don't want anyone to know. Not while Stick isn't speaking to me.

"I don't think I want to go anymore."

"Nope, not an option," she says.

"I mean it, Titi." I don't mean to be mean to her, it's not her fault Mom can't keep a freaking secret. I look down at Kakashi, dying to get to the ending. "I'm just not in the mood for the mall."

"Well we don't have to do the mall but we're doing something." She reaches for my chin and tilts my head upward. "You're speaking to a pregnant woman with two young girls that are truly amazing but also insane and your mom's giving me a pass to spend a Thursday away from them so I'm taking it. You don't have any say in the matter."

Dad yanks Nico from the field, pulling him hard by the arm. It's been thirty-eight hours since the last play.

"Okay?"

I give in. "Okay."

She rubs my head again and I'm not annoyed with her, I'm not even pissed, I almost wish I were a little kid again and she could fix all this.

"I miss my Matty and Titi days."

"Me too," I say and she smiles, her bright white smile and wide blinking eyes. The phone buzzes in my pocket.

"By the way. What the hell is your father doing?" Titi says.

Hey. It's Stick.

It's Stick!

The game's about to start again but no one's paying attention because Mom and Dad are breaking into a full-out war next to the field with Nico in between them. Titi hurries down to help.

The World Is has a concert on Labor Day weekend. You want to go?

Holy shit.

"Matt, get your ass down here, we're leaving!"

I ignore Dad's screaming and text back one-handed.

Yes. Absolutely.

I stare at the screen and wait for the message to switch to "Read." Dad keeps shouting at my mom by the fence.

Cool, Stick texts. **It'll be awesome.**

Holy shit! Stick still wants to see me, or at least see The World Is with me, and Labor Day's a few weeks away but we'll have to set up plans and we'll have to talk to set up the plans so maybe he's okay now and we could get past all this. We have to.

"Get your ass down here before I come up and yank you from those stands!"

Dad steps up on the first metal plank with the vein beaming bright in the dark. I don't know when it got so dark out. I stand.

The game starts again, and the crowd cheers a hit and I tuck Kakashi's Story into my shorts, the Tobishachimaru falling in suspended animation as Kahyo weaves her signs to turn water into ice, the last hope to save them. I glance at my phone, thinking of what to say to Stick to keep him texting, like I want him to be texting, like things are normal between us. I know he's not mad at me, not completely— it's more his Mom, and it's David and Marcus—but he's taking it out on me and it's not my fault that my mom interrupted, he should know that. He needs to know that. He needs to know I want to try again.

"Are you listening to me?" Dad screams.

I'm not. I don't want to listen to him ever again. But I think I should wait, make Stick wait for me this time. I put the phone in my pocket and hurry down the steps.

I will be okay. Everything.

FOURTEEN

OUR AIR CONDITIONER BROKE today, or maybe yesterday, I can't be sure. I couldn't sleep and I didn't dream, and I woke up to the sound of Dad hammering on the back patio, just beneath my window, metal on metal and loud leaden cursing like we're all supposed to be awake at the crack of eleven. I tried to shower but it didn't take so I biked around Woodbridge in the thick of humidity—not the best idea, but Dad's been giving me shit about getting a job and Stick's restaurant isn't hiring so I biked over to Best Buy to apply but you gotta be sixteen to work there and I won't be sixteen until next year. Not that I was dying to sell headphones to freaks with bad musical taste but there aren't many options for a 15-year-old, other than Burger King, which doesn't pay as well. At least at Best Buy you have a chance for something over the minimum and people won't shit on you 'cause their fries are raw.

And I haven't seen Stick. We bought tickets for the concert when they went on sale on Wednesday, but we did it separately—from our bedrooms at the same time—and he isn't texting as much and we're not hanging out at all and it's not like it used to be. I kind of can't wait for this

summer to be over so we can get back to normal—Stick
and me in school and afterschool and everything that was
going to happen between us but hasn't. I miss him.

Mom's still on me about having "our talk," the one about
me being gay or about Stick and me in the basement but I
keep ignoring, refusing to speak about anything really until
I can figure out what happened between us. I jerked off last
night thinking about the concert, the two of us after the
show in the field between our houses, sweaty and touching,
in the dark by the trees past the train. It's sick, I know it's
sick, but it's all I can think about. He just texted me to
come over.

I've been biking like a freak, sweat building then pouring
off my forehead to make up the time between the Best Buy
and Stick's house because it's a far ride all of a sudden, with
a single hand to steer my bike through the traffic. I park
next to the garage, which is open as usual but empty this
time and it's cooler in the shade of the space so I wipe the
sweat from my forehead with the back of my arm but my
cast is soaked, itching and soaked, and my shirt is a puddle
of moisture from my chest to my throat. I should go home
and change but I don't have time to waste. Stick texted me
to come over.

The steps from the garage lead straight into the Turners'
kitchen, a massive space that's twice the size of our entire
first floor and I think I count thirty-eight faces spread
around the long table by the windows singing "Happy
Birthday." Stick is next to Jarrett as he blows out the candles
on a cake baked to serve that many faces. The door slams
behind me.

"Matty!" someone screams, possibly Sammy—wait, is
that Sammy? I step off the steps to move closer.

"Hey, man, where you been?" Sammy says, and he slaps me pretty hard on the side. Some music comes on and it's Rihanna I think, or maybe I think everyone is Rihanna, which is pretty clearly racist, and Rhonda smiles at me. I need to not speak.

"You want some cake?" she asks as I try to catch Stick's attention, but he's laughing with Jarrett and she's pushing me a square of mushed chocolate on a paper plate.

"So you're not even going to acknowledge me?"

I feel a fork to my ribs from behind.

"I mean, here I thought you'd be excited," Cara says. "Do you know I know you?"

"What?"

"Exactly."

Cara's hair is pulled back and looking sort of goth with blue lips and weird eyeliner and I step up to her by the island at the center of the kitchen, trying to get Stick to notice me. David and Marcus are in the corner laughing, but there's no sign of any bushy-bearded guys wielding machetes, which is fortunate.

"Well, you seem distracted so I'll let you be," she says. "I was going to ask about your wrist but that's okay, just eat your cake."

She feigns a move away but I reach to stop her, so abrupt I touch a breast by mistake. I pull back.

"Ohhhkay," she says. "That was weird."

"Oh my god, I'm so sorry," I say, simultaneously turning red and wiping my hand on my shorts … to wipe away the evidence? Sammy runs away.

"You are a really strange kid," she says. She dyed a red streak into the side of her head, above the ear, a single curl purple-red with a beaded gray choker around her neck.

"Let's see the cast. I knew it was broken."

She pulls up my arm to inspect and I spot David throwing a headlock around Stick's neck at the table.

"What did they say—six weeks?"

"Yeah," I say. "Six to ten."

"It'll be six, it looks fine," Cara says.

"Thanks," I say, which is a weird thing to say and I don't know why but she makes me nervous and I just want to see Stick, now fighting back against David with Janice breaking them apart, typical for a family event at Stick's house. Except that Sammy's here. And this Cara girl—I mean, woman. I really need to not speak.

"Oh shit, Matt... come over here," Cara says and she pulls on my arm—the casted one—then apologizes as she pushes me in front of this tall white guy, reaching out his hand to greet me.

"Hi."

His grip is firm and warm or maybe I'm just warm.

"Kepler, this is Matt; Matt, Kepler."

Cara adjusts the choker, which was twisted a bit around her neck, and Janice and Michaela are now punching on David. Stick hasn't looked up for me yet. I wonder if I should text him.

"Are you one of the guys that likes The World Is?" Kepler says.

I look to Cara and she laughs. "I tell him things," she says.

She wraps her arm around his waist and he's really tall and quite handsome, which is exactly how my mom would describe someone so I'm super lame, but my gaydar is flinging alarm bells through my brain.

"Your name is Kepler?"

"Yeah, it's sort of like 'Stick' except, you know, an actual name," Cara says. Kepler laughs. He's white, which is weird because I thought she said her brother was the one who liked the band so it must not be her brother, it must be her boyfriend, and I guess he isn't gay. She has her arm around him, squeezing tight.

"We're going to see them in Asbury," Kepler says. "It's going to be amazing."

"We're going, too!" I shout and I look across to Stick but he doesn't notice. Michaela is hanging off his arm and laughing.

"That's awesome," Cara says.

"Umm ... yeah," I say, toning it down.

"Well well welly well well, we might just have to hang out down there," she says.

"I thought you said you didn't like them—"

"Eh, they're alright. And my brother invited me."

"Brother?"

I look to Kepler and he starts to laugh and my embarrassed face is red again. The music swells from the speakers in the living room and Sammy is dancing by himself.

"Kepler's my brother," Cara says. "Well, half-brother. Same mom, different dad, it's a whole thing. Not exactly Jarrett's family situation, which is insane, but yes, I'm his sister."

"Not just my sister," Kepler says. "She's my best friend." He smiles all corny-like but it's cool, in a way. Cara hugs him sideways.

"Oh crap what time is it?" She grabs at his watch and shouts for Rhonda to come over. Stick looks up and notices me. Finally.

"We have to leave," Cara says.

"Right, right," Kepler says. "Our reservations."

"Yes, so sorry, we have 'reservations'," Cara says, with a fake British accent.

"You're taking Jarrett out for his birthday?" I ask.

"It's not his birthday," Stick says. It's Stick! Stepping up the steps to the counter between us.

"Huh?"

"He's going to college tomorrow, this is his going-away party," Stick says. Jarrett and Rhonda join us in the space between the wide center counter and the cooking part of the kitchen. A few children run past giggling.

"But you were singing—wait … what?"

"I told you they're not that bright," Cara says to Kepler. He laughs.

"No one knew the appropriate song for 'good luck playing football in college' so we kind of winged it," Rhonda says.

"Yo, later Stick," Jarrett says and engulfs him in a massive bear hug as Cara touches my arm.

"Hey, give me your number," she says, pulling out her phone.

"Huh?"

"Número de teléfono?" she says and I hesitate. "Para el concierto? Oh wait, do you not speak Spanish?"

She looks at me side-eyed almost like she's winking at me, or flirting even but there's no way she's flirting. Or is she? Rhonda and Jarrett do their rounds of goodbyes at the table by the window where the rest of the family is eating cake.

"That actually was a little racist. Sorry 'mate," she says, again with the British accent, and Stick laughs as he gives her my number. I feel a surge of delight that he has it memorized.

"See you guys at the show?" Kepler says.

Stick nods and Cara says she'll text me as Sammy steps over to join us. I'm still not sure what's happening. Cara and Kepler follow Jarrett and Rhonda through the door to the garage.

"Yo, when is your family leaving?" Sammy says.

"Soon, I think."

"And then Staci's coming over?"

"Yeah," Stick says, glancing my way, and all of a sudden the confusion spins to panic, instant panic, a swift rush of blood to my face at the mention of her name.

"What?" I say.

"Staci's friend Krystle's been texting me," Sammy says, "and Stick got her to come tonight. She's flicking fine."

"What?"

Sammy laughs. Like always.

I look back to Stick, staring hard so he can catch my eyes, the anger rising behind the panic, coming on so strong that I have to fight to keep from screaming out.

WHY IS STACI COMING OVER?????

"Sammy's been bugging me to set them up," Stick says, like he can read my mind. "I don't know."

This is why he hasn't been texting. He never admitted he was gay, not fully, and maybe he lied when he said he didn't like her and that he really liked me, and I don't know what the shit is happening.

"You should have her bring another girl for Matt," Sammy says. Always helpful. The room explodes as Frank enters— he's one of Stick's older brothers who never comes around, and everyone turns to cheer but Stick is stuck on me.

"I'm sorry," he says. "Cara used my phone to text you. She said she wanted to see you."

I nod but I don't move. I'm watching from above as a laser beam shoots out of Mecha-Naruto's eyes and pierces my skull into thirty-eight pieces. He didn't even want to see me.

"Staci's been texting but we're not back together or anything," he says. "It's nothing."

His lips keep moving but I can't hear the sound and what must be the longest Rihanna song in the history of music shatters the remnants of my brain. Frank calls for Stick to come over and he touches my wrist, disappearing into his family. It's over. It's definitely over. I just want to go home.

FIFTEEN

EVERYONE'S GONE HOME.

Well, not everyone. Krystle's here, this girl from our school, and she's Korean or maybe Japanese—I should probably know or at least not assume because I hate when that happens to me. I'm about as white as a Latino can look but I still get asked if I'm Mexican or Columbian when I'm rocking the Puerto Rican fro and a deep summer tan, I just wish it didn't matter, or that we didn't share a school with the children of Trump voters trying to make America white again. Stick's siblings left the house and Marcus and David are in the garage so we retreated to the living room where Sammy's all up next to Krystle, and Staci's close to Stick, inching into him on the sectional. I'm plowing through my second margarita.

Staci has long straight hair, bleached blonde, and she's wearing an oddly colored shirt, not quite red but not maroon and it doesn't look right, not to me. And I don't know why she's hovering so close to Stick—I mean I think I know why, Stick's in denial and he might even try to date her again, but he should have told me, the least he could have done was warn me, because my brain exploded when

Staci arrived and it oozed down my throat into my stomach, where it's festering. With the tequila.

"You think Bieber's hot?" Sammy says.

"No, I don't know, I guess," Krystle says.

She giggles and closes her eyes next to Sammy, who's been up and down serving us drinks. Staci brought the tequila and they found the margarita mix in the kitchen and I'm alone in the recliner on the other side, drinking.

"He's gay," Sammy says.

"He's not gay," Staci says. "But I don't know, he seems greasy, or dirty. A little gross." After the rest of Stick's family left, he invited Trevor and Gavin over, but Trevor said he was at work and Gavin hasn't responded because he never hangs out without Trevor anyway—maybe the two of them are gay, like they said about Stick and me and it freaked him out, all this shit in his head about his father finding out or all those idiots at school who have nothing better to do than make up rumors that are sort of true, and I can't believe how close Staci is to him.

"What bands do you guys like?" Krystle says. Her voice drifts higher at the end of her sentences, which is annoying, and she's wearing a white beaded dress like a summer dress but way too dressy for this party.

"The World is a Beautiful Place and I Am No Longer Afraid to Die," Stick says, pointing to his T-shirt, jet black with white trees extending from his stomach. "You know them?"

"No," Krystle says.

"Yeah," Stick says. "Most people don't."

"It's a cool shirt, though," she says.

Stick pulls away from Staci but not far enough, it's like she's stuck to him, the light above their heads shining on their faces. Staci's teeth are aligned in a smile, but Stick is hiding his eyes, like he's afraid to face me. He should be.

"Stick's going to see them live," Staci says.

"Oh really?" Krystle says. "Where are they playing?"

"Not sure," Stick says.

The audience on the television is screaming at the end of Bieber's song and Staci sneaks her hand onto Stick's bare leg, quick enough that he doesn't notice, the way I notice, the way she inches her hand up his thigh, close to his waist. Bitch.

"Matt?" Sammy says.

"What?"

"The World Is show. Where is it?"

"Asbury Park," I say.

Staci grabs hold of Stick's hand, yanking it from his lap and yanking herself up until she's almost on top of him, smothering him, and I think this girl wants a punch in her face, like she really wants to get hit by me even though I wouldn't ever hit a girl, I don't think. I take a long drink of the margarita and finish the cup. I might have actually gone insane.

"Matt?"

"Huh?"

"I said 'what venue'?" Krystle repeats, in her grating up-speak. "I go to Asbury all the time."

"I think it's called the Wonder Bar." I scan the table for more margaritas and settle on the tequila by the TV.

"Oh, I know that place," Krystle says. "It's right by the beach."

"Oh yeah? You go to a lot of bars?" Sammy says.

"No," Krystle laughs, elongated and strange, slapping him in the chest like they're a comedy act and I don't know why I'm watching this show. "My uncle lives downtown, so I visit him all the time. They have an awesome beach."

"Cool," Sammy says and jumps up just as I reach the bottle. He pours us each a shot.

"I was there last weekend," Krystle says.

"Aren't there a lot of gays down there?" Sammy says as he lifts his glass to mine.

Krystle laughs again, like what the hell is so funny, and I choke down the shot in one bitter breath.

"Well my uncle is gay, so yeah, I guess there are," Krystle says. "Is that an issue for you?"

"No," Sammy says, coughing after the tequila, and I can't help but stare at Staci's hand near Stick's crotch.

"Okay, good. Because my uncle is awesome and gays are, too," Krystle says.

"You tell 'em sister," Staci says and lifts up her cup as the TV keeps blaring this awful fucking music. Staci's more into Stick than he's into her so maybe that's a sign, the only positive sign, but I can't keep focus, I can't even stand straight, and I look to Stick but he won't look up from his drink—he won't even look at me—and I know I told him I'd be fine if he just wanted to be friends but I'm not fine and I won't be fine and I can't believe he's touching her in front me. He doesn't give a shit about our friendship.

I stumble my way to the bathroom, scrolling past the thirty-eight messages from Mom asking where I am, hoping to find a text from Stick, apologizing for what he did. What he's doing. Right there in front of me. The lights are off when I return to the room and Staci's head is buried in Stick's chest.

When Stick and Staci were dating at the end of the school year, I felt this weird distance between us, not all the time but enough that it tore me apart and ripped out my guts and left them bleeding on the afghan hanging over the couch. It's dark when I return to the room so I have to stare to focus but I don't care if Stick sees me, I want him to see me. I want him to shove her face off his chest, his hands off her breasts. I need him to do that for me.

"Oh my god oh my god, here he is!" Krystle screams at the screen. Staci's legs curl across Stick's knees. I need to leave.

"You okay, man?" Sammy says when I stagger around the recliner to get to the door, all the spinning speeding up all at once, like Mecha-Naruto took my skull and threw it into the blender with the tequila. I look toward Stick. Desperate.

"Matt?"

He shifts in his seat like he wants to get up, but he's stuck beneath Staci, her legs pushed all the way up onto his chest.

"I gotta go," I say but the door won't open or I don't know how to open it and Sammy laughs, he's always fucking laughing, and I can't take this anymore, I can't care this much. I pull the handle and stumble outside.

The heat against my face is immediate and strange, and I bend over the porch to heave. But nothing comes out.

I lurch down the stairs onto the grass where we escaped the bushy-bearded freak and ended up in my basement kissing like it was the start of something, fully everything for less than a week, and I look back to see if Stick is chasing me but he's not, he doesn't come. No one comes. I hear screaming in the garage with David and Marcus, like a fight is starting. I leave my bike behind.

SIXTEEN

You ran away.
You were afraid to make mistakes.
But that's the biggest one you made.
And it's unfortunate.
You hit the road,
Yeah you finally left your home
Somewhere to the west I suppose
And I feel bad for you.

I TOOK THE NORTH JERSEY Coast Line from Woodbridge Station and transferred at Long Branch, which was confusing, there weren't any signs and I was waiting by the tracks about to go back, north to New York City instead of further south to Asbury Park until I overheard a conversation that this was the way to Penn Station, so I rushed down the steps over to the other side because I really am stupid sometimes, like with Stick this whole summer and this whole past year, thinking he might be gay and that he could like me like that, this wasted summer waiting for Stick. Fucking Stick.

He texted me this morning like last night didn't happen, like everything is normal but it's not. Maybe he feels bad and he wants to make it up to me by finally talking to me but when I asked if he was free tonight he said he wasn't and when I asked if he was working he said he wasn't so I stopped asking because I know the fucking answer and I can't believe he's dating her again.

Staci. Stick and Staci. It almost rhymes without the rhythm and I guess he's just decided now that he's going to be straight, despite all the evidence.

Mom suggested at dinner that we have Family Game Night, something we used to do all the time when I was younger, but I'm not that young and it isn't that fun and I told her I had plans with Sammy, a half-hearted lie so I could get out of the house and away from my family. Krystle mentioned how she and her friends go down to Asbury Park on the train from Woodbridge, packing backpacks with blankets and food and enough sunscreen to prevent burning—Asians don't tan, she said—and she was kind of funny, or funnier than Staci. Who is the worst. Like literally the worst human being on the planet. And I know that's mean but she stole Stick from me so I'm allowed to hate her, I think. I can't get it out of my head.

Asbury Park is a town at the Jersey Shore, known for the beach and Bruce Springsteen and its gay-friendly bars, like the one I walked past on my way from the train. I stopped in front, across the street, pretending to play with my phone but kind of watching, looking, because it said on Google Maps that they have live music and drag shows—not that I want to see a drag show, or want to be surrounded by gay men watching me watch a drag show, or even hitting on me and touching me but I kept staring at the front entrance, waiting for something to happen. A gaggle of girls came screaming past and knocked me over almost, like they didn't even notice, and one of them made a comment about Paradise, whether or not they should try to get in, but they were too young and none of this is fun and I sprinted all the way to the beach.

It isn't easy to unfold a blanket with one hand, the drifting sands spilling over the sides as I take a seat near the water. The crowd has thinned this late in the day and I close my eyes to the waves rolling onto the sand, pulling back the beach by inches and feet. I must have set the blanket too close because the spray is touching my toes but I don't have the energy to move it.

Because Stick.

I wanted to go in. To Paradise. I still want to maybe. It's a cool name, just "paradise," like it's some kind of sign, waving me in to join them but I don't have a fake ID and I don't know if they make exceptions for 15-year-olds who got dumped for a girl with fake blonde hair and the personality of a leech. I mean, maybe they'll take sympathy on me, pull me into the crowd and teach me how to be a real live gay guy because that's what I am now, or I need to be, now that Stick doesn't like me and I don't like girls and I'm alone on this beach with nothing to read.

The sun is still bright so I take off my shirt and stuff it under my legs, the wind whipping against my skin. I finished Kakashi's Story on the train—spoiler alert, the airship landed safely and Kakashi's punishment for Kahyo was fair and just, but I don't have any phone service and I didn't bring another book to read. It's empty around me, the nearest are a group of girls on a blanket behind me with a family beside them, a few adults and a smattering of children, smacking each other with plastic weapons for sandcastles, oblivious to everything.

The girls on the blanket next to me start packing up their stuff, sandals and towels and lotions into multi-colored backpacks, chattering away and throwing back their hair, and I can't hear what they're saying with my headphones blaring but they keep looking at me, maybe they're talking about me, hoping to snag a gay boy like Staci did. I wonder if Stick is just pretending to be straight because that's what his father wanted for him, that's what the whole world wants for him, and maybe I should fake it too, ask one of these girls to go out with me. Maybe I've never been this depressed before.

I looked at some pictures from inside Paradise and they were "normal" enough, even the drag queens, I mean I'm a little freaked about it all but I'm okay with being gay—or I will be—I just never really thought about going into a club in Asbury Park with shirtless dudes and their muscled chests and super tight shorts flexed around their butts. It's frightening.

And what if I met someone—what if I started dating someone—would I bring him home to meet my parents? I mean at least with Stick they know him, and they like him—or my mom does, at least, and Dad wouldn't freak. But some dude from Asbury with thirty-eight piercings and tattoos peeking out of his shirt—Dad would lose it. He'd say I'm way too gay to play baseball and I should just join the theater club with all the other faggots at school. Give up on me and sports. Give up on me completely. My last year in Little League, I hit a home run to win a playoff game and my teammates carried me off the field—they literally tackled me at home plate and carried me on their shoulders and it was amazing, jumping into Stevie Ryan's arms when we won the championship two days later, rolling around on the hard dirt ground before rushing the mound in celebration. I miss Stevie Ryan and his short wavy hair. I miss Dad giving a crap about me.

"You should move your blanket."

"What?"

"It's getting wet."

There's a man standing over me wearing a tank top and short shorts, stretching his legs where the family making sandcastles had been. They must have gone home.

"Right," I say. The sun is down but bright on the horizon and I can't really see his face. The girls are gone, too, pretty much the whole line of people closest to the water have vanished. The sand is turning to mud at my feet.

"You okay, buddy?" the guy says, bending down to flex his legs, calves bulging as he stretches. "You're about to get sucked into the ocean."

"Yeah. Umm. Yeah." I don't know why he's speaking to me.

"You don't sound very convincing." He pulls one foot straight up at the knee, his body toned and tanned, remnants of a beard on his cheeks.

"Sorry."

"You don't need to apologize." He continues to stretch for his run. "What are you listening to?"

"The World Is?" I shake my head. "You probably never heard of them."

"Can't say I have." He smiles. "What are they like?"

"I don't know, it's tough to describe. My mom calls it suicide music."

He laughs and the water splashes onto my blanket, soaking the edges. I climb to my feet and shake off the sand, and he helps me move it back from the ocean. "Thanks," I say and I'm pretty sure he's gay, but I'm not sure what to do with that information.

"No problem. And is it safe to assume you're not considering it?"

He forms a slight smile, like he isn't sure if he should be joking. My gaydar isn't that great, but it's just that I'm in Asbury so the odds are great, but he's kind of old, not super old I just don't find older men attractive, like actual men, and he's in his twenties probably, older than Kepler at least and definitely not a teen. Not Stick.

"Are you?"

"What?"

He leans down and a nipple slips out of his tank top.

"You're not contemplating suicide, are you?"

"No," I say, super quick, and my face turns red. I must look like a freak alone on the beach on a Saturday night.

"Okay, that's good," he says, standing up and looking behind him, at the ocean. The sky is lower now with the sun at the horizon. "Because I'm sure if you were, you would tell a random stranger you met on the beach, right?"

He's smiling at me but I can't see his eyes and his teeth are straight and white.

"That was a joke," he says.

"Oh."

"Wow. I'm way off my game today," he says. "Most people find me funny."

"I'm sorry." My feet are wet and sticky and The World Is plays low in my headphones. I don't know why I mentioned 'suicide,' other than my stupidity. I slump my shoulders to hide my naked chest.

"You apologize a lot, you know."

"I'm sorry."

He laughs. "Okay, I get it, I get it—you're the funny one. I shouldn't have tried to compete."

He pulls his elbow behind his back and waits for me to speak but I'm thirty-eight seconds behind the conversation and I keep forgetting to breathe. I pull my legs closer, against my chest.

"Well I'm going to go for a run but if you're still here when I get back, I'll bother you some more, alright?"

"I'm not gay," I say, blurting it out like a total freak and I don't know why, it's not true for one and by the look on his face he wasn't even thinking of that and even if he was, I didn't need to say it.

"Ohhhkay," he says, elongating the vowel and stepping back two steps like he just realized I'm crazy. Legit crazy. "That's okay, man. Wait—did you think I was coming onto you?"

"I'm sorry," I say. One more time. I jump up off the towel, shoving the wet blanket into my backpack.

"Hey, relax, man, no worries," the man says. "I mean, you are cute but you're just a baby."

He laughs, in a super gay way, like he was hiding it before and now he knows he doesn't need to, it's so obvious, I'm so freaking obvious, and I shouldn't be allowed to speak. I don't know how to do this—I mean I know I'm gay but only ever with Stick and our last kiss in the basement was our last kiss forever so I'm going to have to be like this, like him, but I don't know how to laugh like that and I'm not buff like that and there's no way I could walk up to a stranger on the beach and speak.

"It's okay if you're not ready," he says, leaning forward to tap me on the shoulder. "I wasn't ready when I was your age either. You'll get there."

He waits for a response that I can't possibly give then he takes off in a full-out sprint along the sand by the water. I grab my sandals and rush for the boardwalk, cranking the volume on my headphones louder and louder until I can't hear myself think.

I won't be okay. I won't ever be okay. Everyfreakingthing.

SEVENTEEN

I'M OKAY. OR BETTER. Or not as out of my mind / losing my mind / pulled into the depths of depression that crushed me last weekend. It's over. I'm over it. That's what I keep telling myself.

And Stick and me are okay. He apologized for Staci, or at least her presence at Jarrett's party, and he sounded sincere, about as sincere as you can sound via text. He said it was all Sammy's idea and he didn't expect me to be there which I guess is better than the alternative or maybe I've just accepted it. All of it. But he's been texting about the concert and we're one week away from seeing the greatest band that ever existed and I'll be with Stick and he won't be with Staci and then we'll be back to school and maybe things will return to normal, something close to normal, like they were at the start of the summer. That's what I keep telling myself.

Today is Nana's 65th birthday, a good excuse for a celebration, and she had a laugh when she saw my cast, pointing to her left arm, the injured one. She hasn't been able to cook since the stroke so everyone's excited that she's making her world famous rice and my stomach's already rumbling, some thirty-eight hours before dinner will be served.

"Smells good, Mom," my dad says, lingering in the kitchen over the stove.

"Thank you," Nana says, stirring the rice with her good hand, circling her spoon around the edges of the pot.

"See I told you you'd be back making your rice," Dad says and snakes his head around the corner to where I'm standing, a tall glass of liquor in his hand. I'm alone at the dining room table, watching Papa out the window, the tent taking up most of the space on the patio by the pool. My family really does love a tent.

"Did you call Mr. Burton?"

Disembodied head half into my space, like he can't fully commit to an interaction with me. I nod.

"What did he say?"

"I didn't talk to him."

He looks at me confused and the vein starts to bulge, this early already. Dad said we had to beat the traffic to the shore so he made us get up hours earlier than any human needs to be awake on a Saturday. He steps around the wall into the room.

"You just said you did. I don't have the time for this shit today, Matt."

"I didn't talk to him, just to his secretary."

"And then?"

"Then what?"

The table is solid black oak and long enough to seat a dozen people, not quite as big as the one in Stick's dining room and not big enough for Thanksgiving, where the guests number in the thirties most of the time, but it's large enough that he's stuck on the other side with his bulging vein.

"Then you better quit with that goddamned attitude right fucking now," Dad says. "What did the uh—I don't know, the lady, what did she say?"

"Nothing," I say, and he looks like he's about to leap over the table and smack me right in the face, even though he's never hit me, I think the only times I got spanked it was my mother, not him. "She said he'd get back to me, but I never heard back."

I avoided the house last night, I didn't want Dad to ask about Mr. Burton, and I honestly forgot, I really did, it was already five when I remembered to call, and the secretary said he'd left for the day. Stick was working, he's always working it seems, so I ended up at Sammy's and we watched Netflix in his bedroom. He said Krystle stopped returning his texts.

"And did you tell her you were calling about a job? Did you mention my name?"

"Yeah."

"They'll put you on the production floor once your wrist heals, some night shifts and Saturdays. He said you could help out around the office until your cast is off."

He waits for me to say something, maybe even thank him, like I would ever thank him, so I scratch at my cast and stare out the window as Titi walks through the fence with trays of food and my screaming nieces. Dad stomps away with his drink.

Hey guys, trying to figure out the plans for next weekend.

Cara kicks off a group chat with Stick and someone else and my pulse races immediately. Because Stick.

What's up? I say. Like an idiot. Stick hates group chats, and I know he won't be happy he's included but someone needed to speak.

So Kepler has a friend in Asbury who's having a party the night of the concert and he said we could go over after if you guys wanted.

Cool, I say, super lame, and I guess Kepler is the unknown number. I wonder if my gaydar was accurate and if "Kepler has a friend" is code for something else.

Cool bro cool, Cara says and I laugh even though she's making fun of me. **What time does the concert start?**

"Hey kid," Titi says, ducking in from the kitchen after dropping off the food. "How are you?"

"I'm good."

"So Isa got super jealous that we saw that movie. I had to see it again with her."

"Really?"

"Yeah." We watched this Melissa McCarthy comedy, and it wasn't that great but we couldn't stop laughing. Titi made cracks the whole time, and I was dying by the end, I love our Matty and Titi days. "It wasn't as good the second time."

Papa puts the vacuum in the shed and Auntie Luz and Uncle Willie arrive through the gate, weighed down by more trays. We have enough food at these parties to supply half the state so there's leftovers for days. It's not as good the second time.

"You okay?" Titi says, a little lower. I think she knows my secret, and I'm sure Mom complained that I've been hiding in my room all week. She bought me another novel so I've tried to be civil but I'm only a few pages into *Naruto: Innocent Heart, Demonic Blood* and it's not that great. I guess I should have "grown out" of my obsession with Naruto by now, but I've been into it since I was a kid, when I first noticed the manga in the bookstore and I thought Naruto looked cute, this spiky-haired boy who talked like a girl and could defeat the crap out of any ninja who tried to do harm to his village.

"You going swimming today?" Titi says. "It's so hot out."

"Maybe." I did bring my board shorts but I don't really have the energy and I see Dad outside with his drink, stomach hanging over his trunks.

"You should go in," Titi says, "I brought my bathing suit." She pulls down her tank to show the straps of the suit underneath and I smile, we used to swim here all the time.

"He won't go in," Mom says, butting in from the sink in the kitchen. "He's too busy sulking to do anything fun."

"Uh hello?" I say, holding up the cast in case she forgot I can't get it wet.

"I told you we could wrap it up in a garbage bag like when you shower. You could float on one of the inflatable chairs."

I roll my eyes, I'm perfectly fine in the air conditioning. But I'm about to grab my book from the car. It's better than talking to my family.

"Alana," Nana says from the stove, struggling to get out the words. Titi heads into the kitchen.

Hello? Anyone? Hora del concierto? Oh, I'm sorry, Matt's Puerto Rican but he doesn't speak Spanish for some reason.

LOL nope, I say. God I'm so lame. Stick and Kepler haven't joined in and she might be flirting with me. Uncle Willie comes up the stairs in long slow strides with his pile of trays.

Hey guys! I think the concert's at ate. The unknown number chimes in with poor spelling as Willie greets Mom and Titi.

I meant EIGHT. FUCK, my head's in a million places right now.

"Mr. Mateo."

Willie steps into the dining room and I jump out of my seat, I know he won't abide by a simple wave.

"Hey Willie," I say after the hug. Auntie Luz is Nana's sister and Willie is her husband, so I guess he's my grand-uncle—or is it great uncle? Sometimes he scares me.

DUDE YOU DON'T NEED TO SHOUT! Cara texts.

Lolol, Kepler says. Stick is going to HATE this.

Auntie Luz comes up the stairs next, even slower than Willie, and Titi Alana's boyfriend trails behind with several more trays of food. Everyone is excited that Nana is making her rice again and Willie pulls out a chair across from me.

"Don't mind me, boy," Willie says, in that deep halting timbre. "I just need to rest for a second."

Anyway. My friend's throwing a Labor Day blowout that night and it's going to be amazing. Any fan of The World Is is welcome to join.

It's definitely Kepler and I can almost hear him speak through the text, his voice a little higher than most people, or the same as the gay guys on TV. Willie reaches for the jug of wine and searches for a cup.

I'm pretty sure liking that band is a reason NOT to invite someone to a party but whatever, Cara says.

"What are you doing with that phone?" Willie says.

He's my grandparents' generation but he's not as old as them I don't think.

"Just texting," I say.

Meet at the Wonder Bar at 7:30? Kepler says. Doors open at 7.

I hear a loud pop as Papa fires up the grill and a flame shoots out the tent. Nico and Isa are splashing in the pool and the water looks perfect, I just don't want to have to float near the edge with a garbage bag around my wrist.

That sounds awesome, Stick says. It's Stick! **We'll text when we get there.**

"I might have to smack a child one of these days," Willie says, starting on his drink. "All they ever are is on those damn phones."

He doesn't speak Spanish around me like Auntie Luz but his voice is deep and echoing. I don't know if he's ever sat down and talked to me before. It's frightening.

"I'm sorry," I say and turn over the phone to hide the screen.

"Looks like you got something on your mind, boy," Willie says.

"I'm fine. Just making plans with friends," I say, glancing out the window again. Dad jumps into the pool to the delighted squeal of Nico and Isa.

"Yeah. Sure you are." Willie grunts. There's laughter in the kitchen as Nana hits Titi's boyfriend with her wooden spoon to stop him from sampling the rice.

"Only three types of trouble in the world, young man. Money, jobs, and women." He takes a full gulp of the plastic cup and refills the wine. "I know you ain't got money, so that ain't your problem—unless—your parents don't starve you, do they?"

He looks up and I shake my head as he shakes the wine around his cup.

"And you're too young to have job problems, real job problems, like when you're the only Dominican in the plant and the foreman goes out of his way to pile on the shit, because what are you going to do? They'll fire your ass if you talk back." He pauses and holds it there and Mom and

Titi are screaming in the kitchen behind him. "So you just shovel the shit deeper and deeper because your daughter's got to eat and the white devil holds the keys, but that shit burns in you son, it doesn't just sit, and you never forget."

Titi's boyfriend comes over to give Willie a hug and I wonder if this is my chance to escape, like a Shinobi through the window straight down to the pavement because I love Willie, I really do, but I need to see if Stick is still texting.

"But I know you don't have job trouble," Willie says when we're alone again. "And there ain't no school in the summer, so it must be a woman."

I glance at the phone when it buzzes again.

"Yeah, it's a woman." Willie rolls the wine around his cup again. "So, let me give you some advice, son. It ain't worth it. No woman is worth it."

I turn to the kitchen and he grunts again.

"You can tell my wife, I don't care. She knows."

He takes a deep sip and takes forever to swallow and I'm dying to get back to the texts—to see if Stick is as excited about next weekend as I am.

"Not that I don't love her. If I didn't love her, I wouldn't be with her all these years. I don't play with fools like that." He takes another drink and the laughter rumbles from the kitchen. "But it ain't worth worrying about. You ain't gonna figure out what any woman is thinking so don't even try. You understand?"

I nod. Half a nod. I don't have a clue.

"Useless," Willie says and gulps down the rest of his wine. "Listen. What I'm saying is whatever you want to do, do it. If she's right for you, she'll follow. She'll follow. Don't spend your life trying to figure out what she wants. Only leads to trouble. And I got no time to fuck for trouble, understand."

His eyes are hidden underneath his skin so it's almost like he's watching you twice, and maybe that's why I'm afraid of him. But I think I get it, and I like that he's talking to me like an adult. Nico keeps screaming outside like he's completely lost his mind and Mom's laughter from the kitchen is making me lose mine.

"The key to life is this, kid. Only one person in the world knows what's right for you, and that's you. No one else gives a shit." He pours some more wine into his cup and it spills onto the table. "Maybe your parents do but they don't know shit. I known your father since he was your age and he didn't know shit then. Still doesn't. You can take their advice, but they don't know you. That's on you."

I don't know what to say so I just stare, and he glares at me but I'm too afraid to speak. He sets down the jug and lifts himself from the chair. I pick up my phone.

"Like I said," he says, shaking his head and limping away. "Useless."

The messages are jumbled between multiple responses—Stick and Cara then Kepler and Cara then Stick and Cara looking for me. Willie straightens his back and moves for the stairs. I start to type.

Sorry. Family party. Cornered by my uncle. What did we decide?

"Are you okay, Matt?" Mom says, stealthy approach and lower voice than I thought she was capable, standing near me in front of the window. "What was Willie talking to you about?"

She reaches out to touch my elbow, and I recoil at the touch.

"You know, I'm still your mother," she says. "I never said anything about what I saw and I said we don't need to talk about it until you're ready so you really need to cut this silent treatment because it's getting tired. Real tired."

I can smell the garlic on her breath, or the onions, the Spanish cooking seeping out of her pores as she speaks. I don't respond.

"Mateo Luis?" She touches me again and I pull away, shooting back my best impersonation of Willie's glare, all this mothering is more like smothering since she discovered Stick and me. It's not helping. "You're being incredibly rude to me right now."

"Cannonball!" Dad shouts as he dives into the pool, splashing water onto the concrete. I look up at Mom but she's distracted by the screams. I just want her to leave me alone. Why doesn't she understand?

We're meeting them at the concert, Stick says. **I can't wait.**

Mom's still hovering and I'm not sure when it began, my need to keep secrets from her. It's not just Stick. It's everything.

Can you believe we're seeing The World is next weekend. Holy shit!

I check the text and I was right, Stick sent the message just to me.

"I'm sorry," I say, not because I mean it but because I want her to leave. And I am being mean. "Would a garbage bag really work?"

Her face brightens and she pulls back from the window.

"Yeah, I think so," she says. "Let me see where your grandfather keeps them." She taps me on the elbow and I'm back at my phone, texting one-handed as fast as I can.

The world is a beautiful place but we have to make it that way, I say, quoting the lyrics to our favorite song. To

Stick. Then I wait, as long as it takes. He replies with the last line of the track.

And if you're afraid to die, then so am I.

EIGHTEEN

"WE'RE AT THE TRAIN STATION," Stick says, jamming the phone into his ear to shield the sound of his mother's voice. "I don't know, late."

Stick's mother is fighting for custody so his sisters would have to go to court to contest it, which is super expensive and maybe not worth the effort because his mom is likely to win. Especially, now that she's moving in.

"Mom, Mom, just stop! Jesus Christ stop talking."

This is the last weekend of summer and my last weekend of freedom, like for the rest of my life maybe—Mr. Burton got back to me about the job and I'm already assigned to work next Saturday, which sucks, it totally sucks, I won't be able to see Stick as much so this is it, my last chance to convince him about us.

"Oh for fuck's sake, don't even start with the 'Lord's name in vain' crap. Is God cool with you cheating on Dad?"

He hasn't mentioned Staci but he was quiet the entire bike ride to the station and he's been on the phone since we arrived. I need him get off the phone and be with me. It's been so long it's killing me.

"No. I'm not sorry. Were you sorry?"

The train was leaving the station as we sprinted up the stairs, clattering along the tracks away from us. We're alone on the empty platform and the wind sinks into my clothes.

"I'm not having this discussion. I told you how I feel. It's how all of us feel."

Stick is wearing his World Is T-shirt, the one with the black-and-white trees on the front, and I'm wearing the fat black-and-white cat with the ink fading and the edges frayed and I thought it might be lame to show up dressed in their shirts but Stick says it's fine. You're supposed to even.

"No, what I'm saying is if you take Sherry and Aileen to court, me and Michaela will stand before a judge and say you're an unfit mother. Is that what you want?"

Stick balances the phone on his shoulder and pours a long pour of rum into his energy drink, some into mine. He swiped the bottle from his brothers and said he wished he took another. He plans on getting wasted tonight.

"No, I won't be at the house tonight. I'm staying at a friend's." He nods at me and I'm not sure if he means it, if he's lying just to avoid her or he really plans to spend the night with me. Unless he means Staci?

"Now all of a sudden you give a crap what I'm doing?"

Stick's eyes are watering under an open-backed baseball cap, black with "NY" in blue letters on the edge. He doesn't wear hats so he must have known about the wind, kicking up all of a sudden like a hurricane is forming. My hair's a ratty trap of tangled curls, and the clouds thunder in the distance.

"Fine, Mom, whatever. You're right. You're always right."

The heat wave has broken so it's cold on the platform with the sun hidden by clouds. I already know Dad's going to make me set up the tent for Labor Day.

"It doesn't matter, I don't care," Stick says, clicking off the phone mid-sentence—I can hear his mother screaming—and he takes a deep drink from the tall metal can, wincing as he swallows. I'm still holding mine.

"I'm sorry," he says. "You shouldn't have had to hear all that."

"It's alright. What was she saying?"

"She wants me to come home after the concert. She didn't give a crap about me for the last two years but now all of a sudden she can tell me what to do."

He rips open a pastry we grabbed at Quick Chek and texts someone who isn't me.

"That sucks, man," I say. "Are you okay?"

"Yeah, I just can't deal with her at the house right now—especially with her boyfriend there." He chokes down the snack with a pull on his drink. "I don't want to go home."

"You could stay over," I say but I want to take it back as soon as I speak. "Like sleep on the couch or whatever, you know, just so you don't have to be home."

He turns a bit with the wind in his eyes. I don't know what he's thinking.

"Yeah," he says and I don't know what it means but it's all I get and I have to be okay with it. All of it. We can't start the summer again—before his father died and his mother moved in and my mother caught us touching in the basement. It seems like forever ago.

"Hey, so I have something to show you."

He reaches into his jeans and pulls out a baggie filled with blue and white pills.

"What is that?"

"Adderrall," Stick says, lowering his voice even though we're the only ones on this side of the station. "Jarrett left them behind by mistake and he's getting a new prescription sent to school so he said I could have them. I heard they get you high."

"Really?"

"Yeah, I mean, it's not anything amazing but it helps get you up, or pumped, almost like Molly but not as out of control as that. David and Marcus snorted it one time and got super high but I'm not doing that."

"No," I say. Stick never drank as much as he's been and now he's got drugs that get you higher than we've been. I don't know what it means.

"You want to try?" he says, eyeing the pills through the baggie. I shake my head because I don't really want to, I liked when we stuck to the glue.

"Yeah. Maybe we'll see how the show goes," he says and sneaks them back into his jeans. His phone rings but he clicks off the ringer when he sees that it's his mother.

"When are we meeting them?"

"7:30. There should be another train soon," I say.

Stick throws down the rest of his drink and skips the can across the tracks. "So what's going on with this Cara chick anyway? You think she's into you?"

"Noooooo." I flex the fingers under my wrist, beneath the weight of the cast. "She's a senior, isn't she?"

"I think so. I mean—" A few other passengers step up the stairs on the other end of the platform. "Would you ever consider dating a girl?"

"No." I don't hesitate, even though it's something I never said out loud before, or even really thought about, but I tried it one time and I wasn't buying so I'm pretty much settled on liking boys exclusively. I want him to know. "I don't like girls like that."

"Yeah," he says. "Okay." He pulls the cap down, shielding his face from the light, but there isn't much light and his empty can is rattling around the tracks. His phone beeps with a text.

"Is that Staci?"

"No, it's Sherry."

I can hear the train approaching but I don't want it to come. I don't even want to see the band anymore, I just want to talk to him. I sip at my drink and shake my head from the aftertaste.

"What did she say?"

"Nothing, I was just bitching about Mom and she's not really listening. She doesn't think they'll win custody."

He sneaks the rum from his pocket and takes a drink straight from the bottle. I force a longer gulp down my throat. I don't want to wait.

"Are you and Staci dating?"

He looks over and he doesn't flinch, his hands tucked into his shorts and blinking. My mind's in thirty-eight places and the alcohol isn't helping.

"I don't know. Maybe." His face starts to break and I start to break. He tilts his head toward the train down the tracks.

"How do you not know?"

"It's complicated." His face is tucked low beneath his cap and the wind is blowing curls into my face. "I shouldn't have let you see us together. I didn't want you to see that."

"Yeah, well I did," I say. I can't let it go. The train roars into the station but on the other side, on the way to New York. "I like you, Stick, and I thought you liked me, too, but if you're back with Staci I don't know what that means."

Stick watches as the passengers on the platform board the train before the doors close and the train lurches forward.

"I'm sorry, Matt," Stick says. "I don't know what it means either."

"Really?" I say.

I wait for him to speak but he doesn't speak, his head still low. The rain begins to fall in blustery gusts, slamming against our skin then stopping for an instant before starting again. The other passengers rush under cover. We just wait.

"I wanted to try, Matt, I wanted to try this. But it's not going to work. You know that, right?"

"Why?" My can is half full, but I suck up the rest in a single gulp and toss the can across the tracks like Stick did.

"It's too big a secret to keep hidden—it's just not possible. Your mom walked in on us on our first date, for fuck's sake." He's louder now but the platform is empty and there's all this noise from the wind and the rain. "And you said we could go back to being friends. You said you were fine with us being friends."

"Yeah I know," I say, jumping on his words. "But that hasn't happened. You stopped texting like you used to and we don't hang out anymore. That's not back to being friends."

He opens his mouth like he wants to fight back, but he doesn't say anything. Another train lumbers toward the station on our side.

"You're right," he says. "I'm sorry."

The rain picks up again and I shield the cast beneath my shirt to keep it from getting soaked.

"You are?" I say. I need to know.

"Of course, Matt. I am. I'm just freaked out, you know, I don't even know where I'm going to live next week let alone this school year and what happened with your mom really freaked me out and I'm sorry I reacted like that but I did."

The train slams to a stop in front of us. "I just, I could really use a friend right now, that's it."

The doors slide open and Stick steps inside from the rain, but he sees I'm not following so he reaches out and pulls me by the elbow. We stumble up the stairs and I stumble on top of him, my butt in his lap in a seat on the aisle.

"I'm sorry," I say, pushing off.

"It's okay." He laughs. It's so strange that he laughs. "Matt?"

"Yeah?"

He reaches out and wraps his arm around my shoulder to pull me closer.

"I've been a horrible friend and it's not even fair to ask you for this, but I want to go back to being friends again. If you can." He hesitates. "I miss you."

The engine kicks up before the brakes reset and we surge forward, or sideways, and Stick falls against me—again against me, turning to face me like he's about to kiss me. More perfect than perfect.

"Friends?" he says, inching away.

The train winds up to speed and Stick slides over on the seat.

"Okay," I say. I don't have anything left to say.

I will be okay. Somehow. Everything.

NINETEEN

THE WONDER BAR is named for the horseshoe-shaped counter that fills the room at the entrance, long and imposing and shrouded in mirrors, crowded with people queuing up to order drinks we can't drink since we're underage. The guy scanning our tickets said the opening act would be on any minute so we're in a rush to find Cara and Kepler—already inside but in some separate space outside past the stage and we can't quite figure out how to get there. We walk straight for the mirrored walls circling the bar and I nearly smash through the glass before Stick stops me and laughs, we both laugh, it's back to normal between us. Sort of.

"Drinks?" Stick says, pointing at the collection of taps behind the counter. We finished the liquor on the train—well Stick did mostly, but I can feel the buzz setting in.

"Funny," I say.

"I'm serious. Maybe they don't card."

The rain stopped and the sun returned on the walk from the station so my shirt is dry even if my jeans are wet. The opening act is setting up on the stage, tuning guitars and performing mic checks over the sound system.

"Twenty-one to stand at the bar, boys," the bartender tells us.

"What?" Stick shouts, like he can't hear.

"Away, away," she waves, her head half-shaved and severe as her grimace, shrouded in purple lips.

"Come on, hook us up on the DL," Stick says, sliding a twenty across the counter. She closes her eyes for an extended second before spinning to another customer, further down the horseshoe.

"Shit," Stick says. "What a bitch."

"Excuse me?"

She wheels back and waves for security and I grab Stick by his shirt, yanking him away from the mirrors around the bar and then we're fast-walking past a bouncer suddenly looming, so we crouch low against the metal barrier separating the bar from the club, pushing through the crowd until we find an opening to outside, under the covered patio, laughing. It's more crowded outside than inside and there's a DJ playing beneath a big-ass tent. Like the Puerto Ricans took over.

"Mateo!" Cara sneaks over and smacks my chest before I can even react. She might be a ninja. Kepler comes up next to her, his hair shorter and pinker than last time, beneath the lights dangling from the tent.

"Hey Cara," Stick says. I glance behind us for the security guard.

"Hey Stick," she says, her hair sprouting bangs now on her forehead, the red streak on the side less purple than before. "And you are?"

She's looking at me with that smug smile—or the opposite of a smile, I guess. She's wearing a plunging blue tank with a silver necklace.

"Hey Cara." I reach out to shake her hand. She does not reciprocate.

"So why are you boys all furtive and sweaty?" Kepler says.

"What?" Stick says.

"Furtive. You know, to 'furt'," Kepler says and Cara laughs, then they're both cracking up over what I guess was a joke, but I don't get it.

"We pissed off a bartender," Stick says.

"How?" Kepler says.

"I may have cursed at her for refusing to serve us," Stick says and I take a 'furtive' glance around the perimeter, but I don't see any bouncers.

"Yeah. No," Kepler says. "There's no way you're getting drinks here. You're what, sixteen?"

"Fifteen," Stick says.

"Of course," Kepler says, taking a sip from his cup.

"How's your arm doing?" Cara says to me. "Any word from the doctor?"

"No. I haven't been back yet. Supposed to go next week for an X-ray."

"Well it should come off soon." She reaches out to examine the cast. "It looks good."

"Thanks," I say, it's a weird thing to say but I'm not so good in these situations—hanging out with girls who are maybe into me, or guys with pink hair that are totally gay. A roar springs from inside, the opening act coming onto the stage.

"You guys psyched about The World Is?" Kepler says. He's got long sideburns that extend into a thin beard around his chin, light brown not pink, and I think Cara said he's in college.

"Oh my god, yes," Stick says. "I am going to lose my shit. We've been dying to see them forever."

"How long have you been into them?"

"About a year," Stick says, looking to me for confirmation.

"So you measure 'forever' in different units of time than most humans," Cara says.

"You're such a bitch," Kepler says, slapping her on the arm.

"Yeah, I'm sorry. I should stop." She sips on a bottled water and the opening act starts their set. The sound shakes the floors all the way to outside.

"It should be a good show," Kepler says with a weird flashing sparkle like glitter in his eyes. "They're amazing live."

"I know," Stick says. "I mean I hope so." He's as awkward as me in these situations.

"They are, I've seen them four times already. My friends don't really like them but sometimes you crave something different from all that EDM and grind music, this is real guitars and real drums and they're just amazing," Kepler says, elongating the 'a-maze.' Stick laughs.

The opening act continues inside with a steady percussion and a female singer's screaming pouring out onto the patio through the opening. I never been to a concert before, like a real concert—unless school concerts count, which no, they absolutely do not, and I kind of want to be inside.

"We're hitting that party later, if you guys want to go," Kepler says. "My friend has an apartment downtown.'

"Oh yeah?" Stick says. "Cool."

"I'd hold off on the 'cool'," Cara says. "Kepler's got some weird friends."

"Stop, you love Teddy," Kepler says and sweeps his arm around her shoulder, pulling her closer. She tries to resist but she can't quite resist and the rolling-eyed glare that's her default stance fades a bit. Kepler fixes his shirt and lingers on Stick for a second and it freaks me out—stay away from him, you pink-haired freak, he's mine. Kepler smiles at me. I might be overreacting.

"How's Jarrett doing in Maine?" Cara says. "Rhonda's been FaceTime-ing him almost every night."

"I don't know," Stick says, dipping his head beneath the Yankees hat. "We haven't really talked."

Stick always looked up to Jarrett and they used to hang out when he was younger so I wonder if he misses him. I wonder if we were hanging out like we used to he'd tell me things.

"He's probably busy with practice and stuff," Cara says, covering. Stick forces a smile.

"Yeah, there's a lot going on in Maine these days," Kepler says, trying to make a joke but Cara elbows him. He's kind of a dick, I think.

"When are we going inside?" I say. I kind of want to get away from them and see the opening act, screaming out from the stage. The space under the tent is getting tighter, with streams of people squeezing in around us.

"Now," Stick says. "I need to hit the bathroom." He grabs hold of my arm and pulls me through the crowd away from Cara and Kepler, inside with the fans watching the band on the stage. We stay low along the barrier in case security is looking, around the sound system past a couple bouncers that don't seem to notice. Or care.

"Come on," Stick says and jerks me into the bathroom. It's small and dark and he pulls me into an open stall, closing the door behind us. "We need to try this."

His mouth forms a wide grin, close to my face in the tight narrow space and it feels intimate, or it would be intimate if we weren't in the middle of a ranking bathroom with drums and guitars slamming through the walls from the stage. He pulls out the baggie from his pocket.

"Jarrett takes Adderall on the regular so it can't be that dangerous, we won't snort it or anything. I mean, it's medical."

The baggie is filled with blue and white capsules and Stick shakes them in front of me.

"I don't know," I say.

He smiles, in the way only he can, half excited and almost flirtatious, the music pounding from the speakers into our space.

"What if we get really fucked up though?"

"Well that's the point, isn't it?" His lips are close to my lips and someone shouts outside at the urinals, a drunken slur I can't make out. I smell the sweat on Stick's skin.

"Jarrett takes one a day and he never got high off it, just more alert. So maybe we just try two each, okay?" His eyes are blinking and he brushes the swoop in his hair back into place. "I mean, I want to be a little high for the band. And I don't even know where I'm sleeping tonight but we're at a World Is show and we need to be friends again like we used to be because I miss you, Matt, and I miss having fun like this and we need to be high for this, okay? Please?"

I find myself nodding and Stick pulls four pills from the baggie, two for each of us. I'm afraid to try it, I'm always nervous about this stuff, like even the first time with the glue, when Stick convinced me to try, but he's standing on top of me, his face in my face. Someone bangs on the door.

"Yo, hurry up homos, I gotta take a shit!"

The voice is shrill and all this laughter spins through the tiny bathroom but I'm still in a daze from the look on his face when that he said he missed me.

"You don't have to," he says. "I mean, I want you to, but not if you don't want to. Maybe it's best if one of us stays sober."

"Maybe."

The asshole outside the stall bangs on the door once more and I don't know how long we've been in here because time seems to have stopped or gone back to the past when everything was perfect and we were kissing. I hold the pills in my hand, close to my mouth.

"Get a goddamned room, faggots!" the asshole shouts.

"I really do have to piss," Stick says, ignoring the laughter cascading through the bathroom and me standing here, facing him. He unbuttons and spins around to the toilet and I hear the stream before I know what's happening.

I focus on the back of his head, the blonde turning brown or the brown still blonde from the summer sun, more blonde by his ear where it drifts onto his cheek, drops of sweat on his skin. I take a breath and inhale his scent, but I don't want to scare him. I stick one of the pills into my mouth.

It takes like Advil or something equally harmless and I want to swallow it, I want to live in this moment, with the summer almost over and Stick and me together, all the wasted days in the stifling heat when he was avoiding me no longer as pressing. Not now. The asshole outside our door enters the stall next to us and I hear him clanging in the corners of my mind.

Stick flushes and turns to face me, zippering. The pill tastes like plastic on my tongue.

"You took it?" he says.

I nod.

"Cool." He smiles and reaches around me to unlock the door. "This night is going to be legendary."

He pushes open the stall and I wait and watch until he can't see me anymore then I spit the pill into the water circling the bowl. I want to stay sober, a little bit sober, if Stick gets wasted enough to kiss me again.

I will be okay.

Everything.

TWENTY

We are ageless.
Holding our breaths and waiting.
We connect in separate places.
We're all aware of our own purpose.
We all know what makes us nervous.
Just hold my hand
And be my best friend.

SEVEN PERFORMERS FILL THE STAGE at the start. Two singers and a keyboardist, like half a dozen guitarists plus the drummer and a woman playing violin, and the singer is screaming—this short squat dude with a long full beard clutching the mic so tight he might die if he releases, swaying like he's pacing in place as he pauses through a break in the wall of music, this rhythmic swelling soft and slow building, drowning in circles of sound so loud I can't even focus, my head is spinning, literally spinning left and right and up and down as the band lines up all at once in a row and the singer turns spastic now, screaming out loud, shaking back and forth until the drums explode, so heavy and harsh that a mosh pit forges in front of us, right at the edge of us, this girl in restless yellow jeans lifted

above me, carried on waves of hands feasting on the sound
of the greatest band that ever existed.

We agree we're in the same place.
We agree we can't relate
Unless we stay the same age.

We agree we'll stay the same age!

The song slows down and the mosh pit hesitates, the
girl in the yellow jeans lowered back to the ground as the
guitars crawl through an extended verse before a trumpet
appears—from way off the stage, and I think there's eight
in front of us now, more than filling the space because it's
not that big of a stage and this guitarist with long straight
hair almost like a girl's hair—I can't quite tell if he's a girl
or a boy, but their face is covered by hair hanging down the
front as they scream these guttural screams shouting back
to end the track. I may never breathe again.

We're pretty close to the stage, maybe twenty bodies
back, a little off to the right near the bathrooms. Cara and
Kepler are next to us and the mosh pit is contained enough
not to touch us but Stick is itching to jump in with this
frantic energy, up and down bobbing and bouncing into me
like he needs to break free and I should have taken the pills,
I want to feel the way he feels. To feel closer to him.

The audience cheers as another track ends and Stick pulls
me against him, into him, his mouth on my ear but I can't
really hear him, I'm not sure if he's not forming words or
if my eardrums were destroyed by the unrelenting sound
from the speakers but his breath shoots right through me,
all the way down my body, and I can't help but fall, right

into his arms, I think I might be high when the next song begins.

Whenever you find home,
If everyone belongs there,
Feeling our bodies ... BREAKING DOWN!

Stick's arm slides down to my waist and his hand explores the space between my shirt and my jeans and I don't know what he's doing, why he's touching me, but he grabs hold of my belt, tugging at the skin underneath. Cara looks over and shouts but I still can't hear anything, not with the speakers so loud and these urges overwhelming, twisting pulsations into Stick beside me, pressing with his hand on my waist before he spins all of a sudden, these fitful gyrations in half-circles into strangers, rainbow lights filtering above the stage.

"Stick, stop spinning!"

He's lost in his high and singing along to the wrong song I think, and I watch his face, its clear skin and perspiration, this flawless creation, bouncing beside me. I wonder if I kept the pill on my tongue too long and I am actually high or if it's just in my mind but he keeps spinning, this manic spinning, tumbling into me. I hold on.

If your arms are just felt, when you hold me I'll feel held.
We'll sink into these notes.
If your arms become smoke I'll have nothing left to hold.
We'll dissipate with these notes.

I keep my hands on him, both hands and casted wrist because he can't stand up straight, his head is tilted to the side left and right and shaking. There's a break on the stage and the mosh pit settles down again, the musky scent of weed and sweat slipping through my senses.

"This is fucking sick!" Stick screams.

"I know. You won't stop spinning!"

Stick laughs.

"We should go in," I say.

"What?"

"The mosh pit."

I point at the crowd as the next song starts, a slow verse at first but I know it won't last, all their music is just building, slow at the beginning then speeding up faster, guitar licks layered on top of each other with trumpet and drums and that strange violin, alternating singers in perfect rhythm, the musicians lined up again at the front of the stage and swaying in rhythm. Stick pushes me into the pit when the chorus explodes and my body releases. I let go.

Someone knocks into me immediately and the shock slams me into another moshing body but I manage to stay upright, off-balance but upright, and I can't really push back while protecting the cast so I'm lost in the swell of these arms and legs and chests, smashing into me in succession. The beat slows down for a second so I try to catch my breath and I try to find Stick, but then the singer screams out and the guitars spring back and I'm sucked into the violence of all these crashing bodies, losing my balance and collapsing into Stick's side. I close my eyes, so I can feel it inside, these arms and legs and hands pulling at me and slamming into me and Stick's hands are on me—holding onto me, bracing me from these strangers smashing against me, taking over me, and I open my eyes to find his smile. It's everything.

"Holy shit!"

Stick spits into my ear in between songs, the pit coming up for air. "I want to do this every single night," he says, pressing his lips against my ear. "I'm so freaking wired, you know, like my skin is itching but I don't want to scratch it I want to run for twenty miles and live here forever. Oh shit, Matt, what are you feeling?"

He cups the back of my head with his hand, cradling my neck at the base of my hair, pushing my lips closer to his lips, on top of me like he wants to kiss me and it's so loud with all the drums and the crowd that I want to scream out to him, shout out what I'm feeling. I want him to kiss me again.

"This is their last song." Kepler pushes behind us before the start of the next track, I completely lost track. I might be dreaming.

"Really?" Stick yells and I recognize at once, the song that first turned me onto the band, my favorite song and Stick's favorite too, pretty much the greatest song ever written by any human ever. Seriously. Kakashi levels of ninjutsu skills all over these verses. Stick played it for me last Christmas, alone in my basement, and it felt monumental at the time, like all my life after I listened would be different, be better, and nothing that mattered before would ever matter again. Stick wraps his arm around my back.

"This is always their last song," Kepler says and I don't know why but I don't mind. I mean I feel like the concert just started and I wish we could stay here forever but I'm also exhausted and sweaty and shredded by the mosh pit, like I just ran thirty-eight laps after baseball practice and I can hardly stand up. I can't even see.

The song starts with a harsh percussion, this series of spiking sounds loud and abrasive with the singer screaming in the way only he can. I step forward into Stick and guide my hands to his waist. He lets me.

"I'll let you enjoy," Kepler says with a laugh and the mosh pit is swelling and pushing into us again and I want to give in, collapse into him, kiss him hard in front of Kepler and everyone at this concert, convince him what he's missing until he finally gives in.

But he's off into space in his head in that place and I'm alternating stares between Stick and the stage, a series of flailing arms and legs and bodies escaping from the pit and slamming into me, over and over this crashing up and over and I'm holding onto him and he's holding onto me. I forget how to breathe.

The chorus begins so I know we're at the end, but I don't want it to end, this song and this night with Stick's body so close to my body, his arms so tight around my waist. Someone flying overhead launches into us like a Shinobi and I lose my balance, thirty-eight seconds from being crushed in the wake of this massive celebration but Stick hangs onto me, grabbing hold of me despite his space-dream, screaming out the words of the song, the greatest song in history. I close my eyes so that time will stop and I won't need to breathe.

The world is a beautiful place but we have to make it that way.
When everyone belongs here, it will hold us all together.

It's dark inside the club and his arms are wrapped around my waist. I could live here forever.

The world is a beautiful place but we have to make it that way.
Whenever you find home we'll make it more than just a shelter.
If everyone belongs there it will hold us all together.
And if you're afraid to die, then so am I.

TWENTY-ONE

I NEED TO PEE. Like really, really bad. I should have peed in the bathroom at the concert with Stick, but I was distracted by being in the bathroom with Stick. Even more distracted by Stick pissing in front of me, baring everything, and I forgot I needed to pee. Then we were moshing and we started touching and then Stick got wasted, maybe not in that order, but there was a whole lot of touching right out in the open and I don't know what he was thinking but I still need to pee.

Like really, really bad.

Two girls are in front of me waiting for the bathroom. Oblivious.

We walked straight from the concert and it wasn't that far, like half a mile maybe but Stick was wasted, fully wasted, he bummed a cigarette off Kepler even though he never smokes, and his eyes were rolled up in his head.

My phone buzzes in my pocket and I'm tempted to look but Mom's been calling nonstop and I keep avoiding. I sent a text that my phone was dying and I was staying over at Stick's but she won't stop calling. She even called during the concert, but I couldn't hear anything with the music so loud and the mosh pit intense and Stick standing so close to me, touching my skin. The sweaty grip of his pressing flesh.

"What the fuck, there's a line?"

I feel a meaty paw gnaw at my shoulder.

"Goddamn bitches."

I crane my neck at the massive man clutching my arm, his gut testing the limits of his extra-large T-shirt.

"You know what I'm saying?"

Gigantaur chugs a beer and smashes the can in his hand, his eyes raging and breath rancid and I don't know what happened to Stick.

"You need a beer, little man," Gigantaur says, shoving an open can in my hand. The bathroom door opens and two guys come out giggling.

"Jesus Christ!" Gigantaur shouts as the guys walk by without turning. The women laugh and go inside together. Gigantaur snatches at my shoulder and chugs another drink.

"What the hell man, I got to piss with you now?"

Uh, no. No way I'm going into any enclosed space with him. His arm around my neck weighs a ton.

"No wonder these bitches won't talk to me," he says. "Bunch of lesbians."

Kepler's friend Teddy lives here, or that's the story he told us outside the Wonder Bar, out with the crowd on the street too hyped from the night to go home.

Stick followed Kepler and Cara up to the rooftop and they better be taking care of him while I'm stuck in the longest line in history for the only bathroom in Teddy's apartment. Apparently.

"Not that I mean to offend—I mean some of my best friends are gay but Jesus Christ, the chicks at this party won't even acknowledge you." He attempts another sip but the liquid dribbles onto his shirt. "Like make eye contact, bitch. You know what I'm saying?"

I have no idea what he's saying but he won't let go of my neck and he's speaking so loud that the girls in the bathroom must hear him. I shift my weight between my feet to keep the pee from running down my jeans.

"But you got to be 'politically correct'," he says, releasing his grip for the air quotes, spilling more beer on the tiles in the hallway. "I mean, excuse me for liking women because this is America, you know, and I'll be the one who's ostrich-sized"—I think he's trying to say 'ostracized' but he doesn't quite manage and plows forward without hesitation—"because I mean fuck, you can't even leave your house anymore without running into gay dudes and Muslims and people speaking Spanish right in front of you like it isn't America anymore."

The bathroom door opens and I don't wait, I slip in between the two girls—sorry, women!—and close the door behind me. Locking it. I count to thirty-eight at least three times before I finish peeing, and I linger by the mirror long enough to check my face and my hair, a curly mess but I don't have time to fix it, I need to find Stick. And I'm afraid Gigantaur will break down the door if I take any longer. He's gone when I leave the room.

"Matty!" Stick shouts as I push through the heavy door onto the roof. He has a wide-eyed grin plastered on his face, out on the ledge with Kepler and Cara, the party up here more crowded than downstairs. Stick grabs hold of me.

"I thought we lost you," he says. He's leaning against a ledge at the edge of the building, five stories from the ground. "Where were you?"

"Bathroom. Gigantic racist dude almost broke my shoulder. Where are we?"

Stick laughs and shakes his head, straight but not sober. "No clue. All I see is colors."

Kepler and Cara are talking to an older guy with a thin beard and short enough hair that you can almost make out the scalp. Music is blaring from portable speakers and I spy a row of dudes spread out in folding chairs on the asphalt with strings of Christmas lights above their heads and a fire pit at the center—a real-live fire pit shooting out flames in the middle of August. Stick puts his arm around my back, pulling me closer. I lift up a little to pull him off the ledge.

"Are you wasted?" Stick says, super loud over the music. "Why aren't you wasted?"

"Oh. Yeah, umm… I didn't swallow the pills."

"What?" Stick's eyes won't focus.

"I thought one of us should be sober."

His hat is off, I'm not sure when or where he left it but what's left is a disheveled mess tangled from the wind. His eyes make their staggering way up and down my body.

"You know Matt Tirado," he says. "Holy shit that rhymes but—wait I—" He looks at me again and rubs my head, back and forth hard and soft, all at once with his fingers. "You always take care of me."

"Yes," I say. "Always."

I mean it.

"Come over here, Matt," Kepler calls, waving me closer to their group. "Come meet Teddy, it's his condo."

"And my rooftop," Teddy says with a weird fleshy grin. They're sitting on the bricks around the chimney, a little further from the edge. "Not officially but none of the other owners complain about our parties. As long as they're invited."

He winks at me and I look around at the crowd of dudes on the roof—like seriously, Cara's the only female up here and they all have perfect hair and perfect teeth and enough pastel polos to fill an H&M catalog. Teddy shakes my hand and returns it to Kepler's leg.

"So how was the concert?" Teddy says.

"It was soooooo fucking good," Stick says, stumbling over to us. I grab hold before he falls.

"I told you. You should have come," Kepler says.

"You know I don't care for all that indie music," Teddy says, in this odd formal way. "All the bands you like are so obscure."

"Not obscure to us," Kepler says. "Right, Matt?"

"Umm ... yeah," I say, nudging into Stick to make sure he's still awake. He must be wasted not to be freaking. I think every guy up here is gay.

"Oh honey," Teddy says, reaching out to touch my cast. "Where did you find these children?"

"It's a long story," Cara says, and she steps over to help me keep Stick upright. The music gets louder and two of the guys by the fire pit start dancing with each other. Cara pulls open a beach chair for Stick to sit.

"What is he on?" she asks me.

"Huh?"

"What is he on tonight—E?"

I shake my head and I think I need to piss again, or maybe I'm just itching to get Stick alone again, at this party filled with guys touching and dancing, my ragged jeans pressed against my skin.

"What is it then?"

Stick's eyes are alternating between open and closed and his legs are twitching.

"He took some Adderall I think."

"Shit. Addy?"

"I think," I repeat. I don't want to betray him, but I am getting nervous that he took too much and she's practically a nurse, she might know something.

"Idiot," Cara says. She forces some water into his mouth.

"He only took two," I say but Cara ignores me, she's too annoyed to respond. It's dangerous I guess and now I'm worried about Stick, but I can't help but glance at the thirty-eight men now grinding around the fire pit.

"He might be crashing," she says. "We should get him some food." She holds his head back and force-feeds him more water. "Help me."

I try to help but the grip with my wrist is useless and there's two shirtless dudes making out right next to us. My phone keeps buzzing—like for fuck's sake Mom, stop calling!—and I wish I could escape down the stairs with Stick.

"I'll go grab something," Cara says, leaving me holding him up in the chair, his eyes open but vacant. I kneel down on the black tar surface and keep hold around his waist.

"So how long you two been dating?" Teddy says, out loud. He just says it. Out loud. I look to Kepler and he shakes his head.

"Friends with benefits?" Teddy says in that strange formal way. He has a smatter of eyeliner beneath his eyes. Kepler elbows him.

"Stop," Kepler says. "They're in high school."

"Oh, right," Teddy says. "I need to behave." He grabs Kepler's crotch and laughs out loud.

"I said 'stop'," Kepler says, kind of harsh, and the two shirtless dudes grinding nearby might actually have sex right here on the roof.

"I'm just playing, honey," Teddy says and kisses Kepler on the cheek but Kepler's looking at me, mouthing the words "you okay?"

I nod and check on Stick, his head bouncing to the music now, and my phone must be dead because it finally stopped buzzing and I don't know how to get Stick home tonight.

"You been to Asbury before?" Teddy says to me.

"Yeah, last weekend," I say, maybe to impress him. Stick's eyes are open, but I don't think he's listening.

"Oh yeah where at?" Kepler says.

"Just the beach."

"Cool, cool," Teddy says. Someone shouts when the next song comes on—it's like that old Madonna song that everyone knows, so now the whole crowd is dancing, jumping up and down on the sticky tar surface, and I might be the only one at this party who's actually sober. I spot the guys from the bathroom earlier over in the corner, lips locked and shirts off. I wish I wasn't sober.

"There's my buddy!" Gigantaur slaps me on the back and the shock knocks me over. "I brought you a beer."

The sting sinks down my neck, all the way through to the cast. Kepler and Teddy are making up, or making out, and I try to shake the pain away.

"Is he all right?" Gigantaur says. "He doesn't look so hot."

Stick is wavering, shaking back and forth in the chair.

"Are you okay?" I say and Stick finds my eyes.

"I think I'm going to vomit."

He says it with a whisper, or a failed attempt at a whisper, but Teddy jumps out of his seat.

"Bathroom!" he shouts.

Stick slumps forward and Kepler and Teddy get him up from the chair, carrying him arm in arm off the roof to the stairs. I follow close behind, down the heavy steps, and Stick isn't puking yet, but I can hear him moaning, this desperate wailing, everyone rushing to keep the vomit in check as they race for the bathroom. Gigantaur's behind me, shouting about the "whores" at the party, and he grabs me by the shirt, pulling me back to him, but I kick him in the shin with enough force to break free, sprinting down the hall through the door just in time to see Stick's head drop over the bowl.

He's spewing his guts in massive thrusts, this quick steady stream kind of clear not green, and my stomach lurches as the chunks hit the water. I jerk back and spin to the sink, two beats from hurling on my own. Kepler grabs me by the waist, and I steady myself, lifting my damaged wrist to keep a grip on the counter, the other hand to my mouth, to keep it all in.

Stick drops to the floor, crumpled over the mat but he isn't vomiting anymore, he's only wheezing. Teddy pats his back and pushes a towel across the tiles, wiping up the splattered remains that missed the bowl. I hear Gigantaur outside the bathroom, stumbling closer and screaming out my name—or "LITTLE MAN!" but the whole world is spinning now and I need to escape, so I push past Kepler into the hall.

Gigantaur's distracted by a pair of women, so I slip along the hallway in the opposite direction, into a darkened bedroom. I close the door and wait in the dark, breathing deep in the dark, the digits of an alarm clock the only light in the room. The urge to heave begins to fade.

It's cold in the room and I stumble over to the bed, its wrinkled covers soft and forgiving. I let my eyes close for a second.

Maybe longer.

TWENTY-TWO

I DON'T REMEMBER falling asleep and I don't know how long I've been asleep but when I open my eyes it feels like another time and Stick is next to me, under the covers.

"I have to go home, Matt," Cara says. She's watching from a bench at the base of the bed. "Do you want water?" She points to an open bottle on the table next to us, this queen-sized mattress with plush cushions and white pillows and Stick under the covers, sleeping.

"Is he okay?" I say. She must have put him to bed, or someone did because I don't remember doing it and I don't remember falling asleep. I remember he was vomiting, and I remember Gigantaur chasing me and I remember how Stick was touching me at the concert. I don't remember dreaming.

"He should be fine. I got him to eat some leftover pizza and he drank a lot of water, so. He just fell asleep."

Music is playing somewhere in the distance but the door to the bedroom is closed. A television is mounted on the wall above Cara's head. "Sorry about the bathroom," I say.

"Don't worry about it. They cleaned it up."

Her bangs are curled across her forehead now and her eyes look as tired as mine.

"Do you want me to drive you home?" she says. "I'm parked on the street."

"Maybe. What time is it?" I remember my phone, which is definitely dead, and I never texted Mom that we made it back to Woodbridge. She's going to kill me.

"It's three. Teddy said you guys can crash here if you wanted, but I need to get back. I have work in the morning."

"On a Sunday?"

"Yeah, it sucks," she says. "Work sucks. Being an adult sucks. Don't get old."

I laugh, she's like two years older than me.

"Where do you work?"

"Starbucks," she says. "It's tight."

"Wow. Do you know how to make all those fancy drinks and lattes and stuff?"

"Uh ... yeah," she says and she tries to keep her eyes from rolling, the eyeliner smudged a bit at the edges. "Wait, did Matthew Tirado actually ask me a question about myself? That must be a first."

"It's Mateo." I get defensive about my name even though I hate it.

"Oh, sorry." She laughs and touches my leg. I jerk back on instinct.

"Yup, there's the Matt I know. What's your deal, kid? Like seriously?"

"What do you mean?"

She looks over to Stick and I can hear him snoring. A single light in a frosted globe above the bed brightens the room.

"You're a bit ... umm... what's the word I'm looking for—really awkward?" she says. "Do you ever just ... relax?"

"Sometimes," I say but she keeps staring and it's unnerving. "You're a bit … umm … what's the word—really mean?"

The glare of the light hits her eyes and for a second I think she's going to jump across the bed and punch me in the face but then she breaks. Laughing.

"Okay, okay, you got me there," she says. "You can play."

I sit up, looking over at Stick on his side, wheezing through labored breaths. I didn't know he snored.

"So, can I ask you something, Mateo Tirado?"

"Sure," I say.

"You know Kepler is gay, right?"

"Yeah." My face turns red, immediate as fuck.

"And you know he's my brother?" The music down the hall has faded, maybe the party is ending. "And I remember when he was your age. Struggling with coming out."

I dip my head to try to will the red from my cheeks.

"Do you get what I'm getting at?"

I shake my head. I do, but I don't know why she's bringing it up and I'm not ready to talk about it. Not now.

"Oh my god, Matt—don't you have any girlfriends?"

"What? No," I say, offended at the suggestion. Or confused. I don't know what's happening. "Wait … what?"

"No, I mean—no." She laughs. "I know that you don't have a girlfriend, that's the whole point. When I saw you at that horrible party Rhonda dragged me to and I saw the way you looked at Stick, I just … god, it's like I'm drawn to wounded animals that should really be put down—you should really be put down." Her eyes belie her frustration but in a way that's welcoming somehow. I'm not sure how. "So like I don't—I really don't want you to do anything or tell me anything you're not ready to talk about—I mean, everyone's got their own pace and I can't even find a boy in the greater Woodbridge area worth a second of my time but I'm just saying, you should really have a female friend to talk to about this stuff. That's like 'Gay 101'."

She steps over to the bed to prop Stick's head on the pillow, choking for breath at the edge of the mattress. She turns back to me.

"Do you have anyone to talk to, Matt?"

I shake my head.

"Well you do now," she says. "I really wanted to warn you about the party tonight—that there might be a lot of gay guys here, but I didn't want to scare you. Or Stick." He starts to snore again. "Does he know?"

I don't respond, my mind is spinning thirty-eight ways in every direction, like okay, she's known all along that I'm gay which means I'm obvious, I mean Stick and me were pretty obvious at the concert but she knew before that, when she first met me, and I guess she wasn't into me then which makes more sense now that I'm processing, but how did she know? Am I really that obvious?

"Wait—have you two?"

I nod. Her eyes are bright and begging me to speak.

"It didn't end well," I say.

It didn't. Unless we're still in the ending. And she's right about talking to someone. I mean, tonight's been great— better than great, more perfect than perfect, but it might have been the drugs or the Red Bull and the rum and he never seems to want me when he's sober.

"Oh honey," she says, reaching out to touch my leg. "I'm sorry. Do you want to talk about it?"

"Nope," I say, shaking my head so hard that the red melts away and is replaced by a dizzy brown. "I'm good."

She laughs. "Yeah. Okay."

I pull my foot back. Awkwardly. I'm not ready to talk yet. Not about Stick. Not when he's next to me under the covers.

"Well like I said, you can crash here. I think Teddy and Kepler are awake somewhere and you have my number if you need it. Don't call me though, I'll be sleeping." She backs away from the bed, picking up her purse. "But we'll hang, okay? We'll talk."

"Okay."

"I'm serious," she says. "I mean if you need to talk right now, I can always be late for work. Starbucks ain't shit."

I laugh. We really do need to hang out. She's kind of awesome. "I'm okay," I say and I think I am, I think I just came out again. And this was light years better than coming out to my mother. Actually, if I include Stick and Titi and Kepler and Teddy, that's like thirty-eight people that know about me and the world hasn't exploded yet so maybe I'll survive this.

"Awesome," she says. "You know I don't believe you, but I'll let you be."

She smiles at me. She never smiles. It's nice.

I push myself closer to Stick when she leaves, eyeing the covers and the soft white pillows. His eyes are closed and he's snoring louder, the back of his head propped up so I can see his face, soft and smudged and hair out of place, sweeping down across his forehead.

I will be okay, I say, out loud this time.

I could stay here forever.

TWENTY-THREE

STICK PITCHES FORWARD like he's under attack, scanning the room for a few frantic seconds before finding my face. He sits up on the pillows. Next to me.

"What time is this?"

"I don't know," I say, blinking hard in the lights. I might have dosed off while watching him. Waiting.

"Where are we?"

"I'm not sure. Are you okay?"

"Yeah, I just—" He shifts on the mattress to push himself up, but he's trapped under the covers. "Help?"

I laugh and clear the covers off him, his face pale and his hair a mess, matted down and stringy.

"I puked?" he says. I nod. "Damn. Did I do anything crazy at the concert?"

He lets his head slump into the wall behind us and points his eyes at the ceiling and a bit of panic rushes through my head—doesn't he remember the touching and the holding and the grabbing and the hugging, in the pit and after the pit.

"You don't remember?"

"A little. Mostly."

He closes his eyes and I wait for him to speak, half-awake on the bed next to me.

"Thanks for watching out for me."

"Of course," I say and start to touch, but I switch it to a bro-tap on his jeans.

"Always."

The party's over, it's been quiet for a while now, an eerie silence through the apartment before I fell asleep. I haven't eaten since pizza before the concert and my stomach starts to rumble beside him.

"You're not still high, are you?"

"Maybe," he says. "A little."

"What does it feel like?"

"It's strange. Different than the glue. It's like my head is ahead of itself or my mind is just spacing and I can't really place it. It almost feels like I'm in motion even though I'm not moving. We're not dancing, are we?"

"No. No dancing."

He smiles and looks down from the ceiling at me. This is everything.

"We should play some tunes," Stick says and fixes his phone to play The World Is, some of their older music, this perfect music, but all of their songs are perfect to me.

"My phone died," I say.

"I'm under 20 per cent. Maybe I should save it, in case we need it."

"Maybe."

We let it play for a bit and I try to clear my head for a bit. I can't tell how sober he is, if he'd notice if I touched him.

"You think they have a charger in here?" Stick says and turns too quick, losing his balance. I feel the heat of his body as he brushes my body.

"I haven't seen one. I'm a little afraid to read the thirty-eight messages my mom left since we left the concert."

Stick laughs and nudges me in the side. This is perfect.

"I love this song. They played it tonight, right?"

"Yeah."

They did, I recognize the drumbeat spilling from Stick's phone, resting on the covers over his legs. His eyes begin to focus and his skin is glowing in the globe above the bed.

"So umm … Kepler… super gay, right?"

I nod. I guess he noticed.

"Yeah," I say. "I think so."

"Okay."

I clamp my teeth against my lips to keep from speaking or reacting. I need to know what he's thinking.

"I got that vibe the first time I met him," Stick says. "But he seems cool."

He looks up at the ceiling again and I wait for him to speak but his lids are fluttering like he's about to drift off again.

"You want some water?" I don't want him to fall asleep, now that he's okay with Kepler being gay. I point at the table where Cara left the water. I think it's empty.

"Nah, I'm good," Stick says. "Is the party over?"

"I think so. Kepler and Teddy must be sleeping, or—" I stop myself before I finish the thought and my cheeks turn red as fast as I speak.

"Oh yeah, they are very much not sleeping right now," Stick says with a laugh. It feels okay to laugh.

"I'm starved," he says. "Is there any food left? Or alcohol? Wait, no, I don't need any more drinks tonight."

He looks at me and studies my face and I'm so sick for thinking this, wondering how I look to him and if he's looking at me like that even though he said we couldn't do that anymore. He just wants a friend. He closes his eyes.

"You know, my father never drank. He should have, when you think about it. He would come home every night exhausted from the construction site, like every day someone screwed something up that he had to fix and then he'd come home and deal with us kids and my mother." His eyes blink open and he readjusts the pillow behind him. The paint above the headboard is chipped and peeling.

"Did I tell you the time I went to his site and he forgot about me? I mean, not completely but he got called off the job and he figured he'd be right back, but he never came back. I was just sitting in this trailer playing my Nintendo DS." He pauses, scratching at his jeans. "And I didn't have a phone then, and I didn't know where he went and I got so scared I started screaming and one of the foremen found me. But I freaked out and yelled at my dad, like the only time I ever yelled at him. I couldn't believe he left me."

He lifts up the water. The bottle is empty.

"I miss him, Matt. I can't believe how much I miss him."

"I know, Stick." I drop my hand onto his leg.

"And I just want to make him proud, you know. I don't want him to worry about all this crap between Mom and me and the custody. He shouldn't have to worry about me. Maybe I should just accept it, you know. Stop fighting."

"He wouldn't want that," I say. "You know he wouldn't want that."

"No." Stick says, shaking his head. "He hated that bitch." I start to laugh but Stick's not laughing. "Can you believe she's at my dad's house right now with her boyfriend, her freaking boyfriend—I mean who does that?" He slams his head against the wall so hard it has to hurt. "I fucking can't with her, I just can't."

He reaches behind him, wincing, and I want to hold him, just to comfort, nothing else, but he wouldn't take it that way and I don't know if I mean it that way, glancing down at the covers, wanting to be under them. What is wrong with me?

"I'm sorry," I say. It's all I ever say.

"It's not your fault, Matt. It's nobody's fault." He pauses and tosses the empty water across the room. "No, I lied. It's her fault."

It's bright in the room from the single light overhead and I notice the flat-screen on the opposite wall has a crack, off to the side, not on the screen itself but in the black metal that protects the borders, this fault line running halfway up and wide enough to notice.

"I'm not going to that house tonight," Stick says, swiping his hair left to right. "Can we stay here?"

"Sure. Cara said it was okay."

"Cool," he says and points to the bench underneath the flat-screen.

"What?"

"One of us should sleep there, right? Just because, I don't know, so there's no confusion."

His eyes are blue, free of the red and the gray from the drinking and the drugs. My skin sloughs off into a puddle beneath the covers.

"I mean, or it's fine, we can both sleep in the bed," he says, covering. "I just meant if we were choosing I should be the one who gets the bed, you know. After the vomiting." He flips half a smile in my direction, from the corner of his eye. "And my father died."

"True, all true," I say. "But you did tell me that you've been a horrible friend so maybe I should get the bed—I mean, that's what you said."

I stick it out there like a joke and I hope he takes it like a joke. I think I'm joking.

"Sure, sure. Throw that back in my face," he says.

"Of course," I say.

"Okay, what about this?" Stick says. "Whoever earns it gets the bed."

"Earns what?" I say and it's too late to react—he shoves his hands into my side and pushes me to the edge of the mattress but I grab hold and fight back and then we're wrestling, flailing at each other for several silly seconds, out and between the covers, and I roll on top of him, clutching and grabbing at his shirt and his skin.

"Ahh!" he screams because I'm punching on him and he can't defend from underneath the blankets, laughing like he's crazy until he's no longer fighting back, he's letting me punch him until I'm no longer punching, I'm just touching. He's letting me touch him.

I find his eyes and pull back a bit. Afraid to keep touching. I wait for the seconds to pass like hours that pass like years that I've been waiting. I let his hands escape from under the covers.

He grabs me by the waist and yanks me into him, and the kiss is so quick I catch chin not lip before drifting, just enough to gauge a reaction before he squeezes my back with his trembling arms and pulls me into him. Longer and deeper against his lips, my chest on his chest and my legs around his legs, clutching tighter. Kissing.

He moans—I hear him moan—so I press deeper, using my good hand beneath his shirt to his skin and I open my eyes to see his eyes, open and bright in the light above my head. He wants me to.

I lean in, grinding at the waist, my hand under his shirt. Breathing him in. I want to rip off the cotton and claw at his skin, dig underneath until I touch his insides. His eyes are closed, and his lips are warm and perfect.

I can't hear the music so his phone must have died, and I let my fingers wander below his stomach to his jeans. Time stops and my mind stops, it's like I'm watching this image on the television screen, the cracked black metal splitting open and swallowing me whole when I reach beneath his jeans and find his boxer briefs. I close my eyes and touch.

"Matt, stop," he says.

He pulls my hand from inside his jeans and pulls himself out from under me, scrambling on top of the pillows. I'm half sitting, half slipping off the edge, and he curls his legs up to his chest but I'm thirty-eight seconds behind his mind so I press forward, pushing closer, and he slaps my arm away.

"Matt, stop," he says, louder now. I stop.

Neither of us is moving, we're sort of frozen in place but not quite frozen and my brain is too broken to even attempt a reaction.

"Matt?"

I look up and see that he's pissed, and I'm so confused I don't know why we stopped.

"Get off of me," he says and punches me in the chest and I fall back to the mattress, about to drop over, gripping tight with my cast and losing balance fast. He scrambles over the covers to the other side.

"You're sick, Matt, you know that! You keep making me do this. I'm not fucking gay!"

He spits out the words like bullets through my skin. The pain begins to set in.

"This is over," he says as he staggers to the door. "We can't hang out anymore." He's shaking his head and crying. "I just can't."

He pulls at the knob and pulls the door open and the pain in my cast spikes through my wrist until I lose my grip, falling from the mattress like the airship Tobishachimaru, one quick drop from the bed to the carpet and I can't brace for impact. My face slams into the floor.

"Ow," I say, or something equally useless, and I try to stand but my wrist doesn't work and my legs are too numb to lift my body. I feel the blood trickle onto my chin.

I can't hear anything from the hall but everything's fuzzy all of a sudden and my head is ringing. The blood slips down my lips and drips off my chin onto Teddy's carpeting. Stick is gone and he isn't coming back. The pain is overwhelming.

TWENTY-FOUR

MY LIP IS ENGORGED, blackened and burnt with specks of blood caked onto the skin, and there's a cut inside, deep and red and bright, I must have bit down when I slammed into the carpeting. I cleaned my face in Teddy's bathroom and tried to find Stick but my phone is dead and he wasn't at the station. It's light out now or the sun is coming out, but it's cold as hell in the wind on the platform, waiting for Stick to show. He doesn't come and his bike is gone from the racks at Woodbridge Station.

Stick and I started biking to school together last fall—I'd pick him up in his driveway or wait in the garage if he was late, and his father would always say 'hi' to me on his way to work, more than my father ever did. And I didn't mind waiting for him, I mean half the time we'd risk our lives dodging traffic across the highway and we'd still miss the last bell for homeroom. But at least I was with Stick. Every morning me and Stick. I won't ever do that again.

It's over. It needs to be over. I can't take this anymore, it's too much—the waiting and the hoping and getting everything I ever wanted only to have him pull it back and stop speaking to me. Again. I think about biking past his house next week without waiting for him. I can taste the blood in my mouth.

"Where the hell have you been?"

My dad is standing in the doorway. Blocking the entrance.

"Stick's."

"Bullshit. Your mother called there last night, and they said Stick wasn't even home."

He won't let me pass, his thick body filling the gap in the doorway, and I step back down the steps, the wheels of my bike spinning in the grass on their side.

"Is that Mateo?"

Mom calls out from somewhere behind him and my phone is so dead I don't even know the time except that it's morning and I'm tired and I've never been so happy to hear her voice.

"Where the hell were you?"

Dad glares at me like he's about to hit me and I almost wish he would, just slap the crap out of me so I could focus my anger on him.

"Mateo!" Mom tries to inch around him but he won't move so she just bangs right through onto the porch. "Thank god you're all right! What happened to your face?"

Nice of her to notice.

"It's fine," I say, brushing her hand from my lips and Dad moves aside so I can step inside, sticking an elbow into my ribs. I collapse on one of the chairs in the entry room. Both my wrists are throbbing.

"Where were you all night?" Mom says. "We were worried sick."

They gave me permission to attend the concert but I was supposed to call right after and we were supposed to come home last night. I wonder if they waited up for me.

"Your mother asked you a question," Dad says, not waiting for an actual answer. He's hovering over me, in his Brew Fest T-shirt and shorts, and I almost feel bad that they were worried if it weren't for all the hate. Mom steps beside him, as annoyed as he is.

"We got stuck in Asbury after the concert and missed the last train."

"You've been in Asbury this whole time?" Mom says. "Why didn't you call us?"

Dad backs away, like he's already bored with the conversation, so Mom takes his place leading the interrogation. I look from her to him and back to her, like I'm a little kid again, bringing home a bad grade.

"My phone died," I say and show her the dead screen. "I told you that."

"You couldn't find another phone?" Dad says. "Stick doesn't have a phone?"

"His died too," I say and I kind of can't lie—I mean I'm no good at it, I feel my face turning red and I look down at my feet, a dead giveaway, so I look back up at him, abruptly. "The concert place had such a weak signal it drained our batteries."

I'm hoping a technical explanation might confuse them—they suck at technology—and I wish they would save all the questioning until after I get some sleep or some food at least, I need to charge my phone so I can text Stick, even though he won't answer and I know I shouldn't text him, I said it was over and I need it to be over and I shouldn't want anything from him. But I don't want it to be over yet.

"Where did you go after the show?" Mom says. "How did you miss the train?"

I sink deeper into the chair as Dad shifts forward and I

can't even think what to say at this point because the truth is not an option and they aren't buying my only lie and I just want to sleep.

"I don't know," I say. Just punish me and get it over with, nothing they can say will be worse than losing Stick.

"What do you mean? Where did you go?" Mom repeats. "And what happened to your face?"

"I'm not sure. The concert got a little crazy." I look up. "I think I got elbowed in the mosh pit."

"Mosh pit?" Dad says. "You were in a mosh pit?"

"Yeah."

He sneers, like he can't quite believe it. He doesn't even know me. Asshole.

"We should put ice on that," Mom says.

"He's fine," Dad says. "And there's no way he got that at the concert. It's way too fresh."

"What?"

"We'll be here all day until you stop lying. Is that what you want?"

"No." I shake my head and look back in defiance.

"'Cause I got a ton of shit to do to get ready for your mother's family and I don't have time for this crap."

I see the vein emerge at the side of his head, but he's not really pissed, it's not even pulsing, he just doesn't want to deal with this. I forgot about our Labor Day party.

"Did you get in a fight, Matty?" Mom tries, stepping closer to me, leaning down on the carpeting.

"Yeah," I say. I give up. I just want to sleep. "I guess."

"With who?" Dad says.

"It doesn't matter. Can I just go to bed, please?"

I stand up and make a move to move away from him, but he latches a heavy hand on my shoulder.

"Jay!" Mom tries to jerk him off of me, but he brushes her away.

"We're still talking," Dad says, pressing all his rage into my arm, so intense I want to wince, but I don't want to give him the satisfaction. "Either you were in a mosh pit with your broken wrist because you don't give a shit about baseball or your future or someone gave you a fat lip this morning. So which is it?"

He twists his fingers into my shoulder, and the pain starts to pulse like the vein in his head and I want to reach out and strike him, ninjutsu attack straight to the temple, see the blood spurt all over Mom's carpeting, for everything he's ever done or said or the fact that he doesn't give a shit. He pushes me back into the seat like a piece of garbage.

"You want to know the truth?" I say.

"Jesus Christ, what the hell do you think I'm standing here for?"

I don't know why he hates me so much. I don't know if he thinks Mom favors me over him—that's flashing through my mind for some reason, that he's just jealous, a fat jealous jerk who's always hated me no matter what I've done and he's way too strong for me to try to punch, to smack that stubborn sneer from his face and make him cry like me. For once.

"Are you going to speak or just sit there all morning and do nothing? Like usual." That vein in his head is about to explode. I watch it pulse as I say the words.

"I'm gay."

"Excuse me?"

"Stick and me were kissing and he got pissed that I touched his dick and I fell off the bed and hit my head."

"Oh my god," Mom says.

Dad just stares, expressionless, or the same exact expression, and I focus on the vein to see signs of the impending break, the rupture that will cause a seizure and it'll be sick when I celebrate.

"What do you mean kissing?" he says.

"I'm gay," I say, loud and proud all of a sudden, into his fat ugly face. Then, more quietly, "Mom knows."

"But I thought you said—" Mom says.

"Wait, you knew about this?" Dad turns his anger to her and I have a chance to catch my breath. I need to catch my breath. What did I just say? I can't breathe.

"Relax, Jay. Let me talk to my son."

"He's my son too," Dad says. "Are you and Stick—wait, what are you saying?"

I laugh. All of a sudden some laughter escapes, in the place of my breathing, because I've gone insane. I'm completely insane. I just came out to my parents and their reaction is, I'm not sure but I feel like I'm floating in space outside of this place, watching their reaction, and I laugh, I have to laugh. Dad backs off like he knows I'm insane.

"Mom. Dad."

I find myself rising out of my seat like my chakra's been unleashed because I didn't intend to stand, and I don't know why I'm speaking.

"I'm gay and I'm in love with Stick and we kissed last night and we had kissed before but he isn't gay, he has a girlfriend now, so it doesn't matter now, he freaked out and knocked me off the bed and I hit my face and my wrist. Then I walked to the train station and he was already gone and there wasn't a train so I caught the first one to Woodbridge. I'm sorry I didn't call. I just wanted to get home."

"Oh Matty," Mom says and steps forward, reaching out to hug me. I don't even care that she called me "Matty."

"It'll be okay, sweetie," she says, and I wish I could take it back already, that this wasn't all out in the open but it's here now and I can't stop the tears from starting.

"How long have you known?" Dad says, to me I think but he's so distant and I don't want to face him.

"I didn't know for sure," Mom says. "A few weeks ago, I walked in on him and Stick—"

"Where? Doing what?"

His tone is harsh, but it's directed at my mother. Because he's an asshole.

"For Christ's sake, Jay, can't you see your son is crying?"

Mom pulls back enough that he can see me, and I drop my head to avoid his eyes but I can't help but sneak a peek, searching for that vein. He wavers.

"Yes. Of course." The sun pushes through the curtains into the room, breaking against my face in a way that almost calms me. "I'm sorry, Matt."

He steps forward and reaches out, shaking my shoulders sort of soft but rough, and it's confusing, like he's the coach comforting me after we lost the game, which makes me angry again, all this rage building up to breaking but it's not enough and this is tough and I look up with as much fury as I can direct at his face.

"You're sorry you have a gay son?"

"No," he says. "No."

He looks down at me hard and reaches out to grab my hand. The pain in that wrist isn't so bad anymore.

"It doesn't matter to me, Matt. Not one bit." He pulls me in close and hugs me, harder than I think he's ever hugged me before, strong and stiff and tense and weak and I fall into his arms with the weight of it all. He holds me up.

"Oh Matty." I hear Mom as she wraps herself around the back of me so it's Dad in the front and Mom in the back, just hugging. Fully even. I almost laugh, or I think I should laugh. Puerto Ricans do love to hug.

"What's happening?"

We break the embrace all together at once with Nico in his pajamas on the bottom step.

"Is Nana dead?"

TWENTY-FIVE

THE AIR CONDITIONER BROKE AGAIN. I couldn't sleep, not with that much heat pressing into my bedroom and the salsa blaring through my opened window, praying for a breeze that hasn't come, my mattress sweat-soaked and empty, wet cat T-shirt ripped a little more and wrists sore, both of them. My phone is charging in case Stick texts but he hasn't—he won't—and I just keep checking because I can't really sleep, and my cast is itching all the way down to my shirt.

We're having a party for Labor Day—full tent and the usual family invites and I was excused from the prep because of no sleep and the swollen lip and the somewhat major revelation I started their day with, which yeah, I'm not sure how I feel about it yet, I almost feel nothing, or the exact opposite reaction I expected after coming out to my father. He didn't freak which is good but I'm not even sure what he said. At least I didn't have to help with the tent.

I throw on a clean shirt from one of the piles on the floor—half-hearted with the sniff test because I need to shower but the house is filled with relatives and I can't risk one of my aunts stumbling into the bathroom by accident.

I slap on a baseball cap and head down the stairs past a bunch of cousins watching television into the kitchen, oddly empty. I do a drive-by on the stove—Nana's rice, black beans, and a plate of tostones that I sneak a snack from before heading out onto the patio. Dad's been replacing the shed this month and it's more like a shell than a shed now, three walls and a roof with nothing inside and no door yet. I climb in through the opening, checking the phone one last time for Stick. No texts.

Dad has a bench set up to cut wood—a makeshift sawhorse with flattened edges connected by a wide board so I take a seat, I need to sleep, I'm half-awake in this weird half-dream in the heart of a party I'm not attending. I feel like a Shinobi, lurking around unnoticed, senses alerted to escape this place if anyone asks about Stick and me but I don't have spiky hair and I don't know ninjutsu and no one is looking for me, not now. I close my eyes and try to sleep.

I hear Nico screaming past, he's always screaming past, and my eyes are closed so I can't tell for sure, but I think he comes into the shed. I'm off to the side in the shadows and I hear a knock on the beam above my head and I'm about to shout for him to leave but I hear Dad's voice first.

"Matt, you in there?"

"Uh, yeah," I say, and he peeks through the opening, shrouded in light.

"What you doing, buddy?"

He never calls me buddy, like not even as a kid, and I think for a second he thinks I'm someone else, someone he likes.

"Nothing."

"How's your lip? Did you ice it?"

"Yeah," I say, reaching up. The swelling's gone down but it's still bruised and bloated. Mom got me some ice before I went to bed.

"Nico said you were in here." He steps through the opening, admiring his work. "Did you get enough sleep?"

"No," I say. "It was hot."

"Yeah that goddamn repairman did a real shit job for all the money it cost me." There's the father I know. "I was thinking we could have a catch."

"A catch?" I lift my cast in the shadows.

"Yeah, I know, I'm not an idiot." He lifts up a white disk. "I found a Frisbee when I was cleaning out the old shed. You only need one hand."

"Oh," I say. We used to play Frisbee on the beach when I was a kid, me and Dad and Nico and Mom sometimes but it's been a while. Forever even. I miss it.

"Yeah, so if you're up for it, just meet me at the side of the house." His mouth forms a weird unnatural smile, like why is he talking to me like this and why is he smiling. "Okay?"

"Thanks," I say, like it's something I should say because I can't really process what's happening—last night I was in a mosh pit then I was on a roof in Asbury with gay guys dancing around me then I almost had sex with Stick but this is the strangest moment of the weekend.

"I don't care, Matt," Dad says, half in and half out of the shed, the sun beating at his back. "Whatever makes you happy, I don't care about the rest of it. Understand?"

"Thanks," I say because words are confusing to me. What is he saying?

"Your mom had a friend in college who was gay—I don't know if she told you that. He was really cool but I think he moved to California or Colorado or somewhere out West but you know, he was a good dude, we used to hang out." Dad steps forward a bit and he's talking normal, like this is normal. "I just … don't be afraid to be yourself, okay? Around me especially. I'm fine with you being gay. I'll even march in a parade if you want."

Damn. He's starting to make me emotional. I almost want to forgive him for everything. I nod and he's still smiling. I choke back the tears.

"I promised Willie I'd take a look at his engine," he says, "but I'll meet you by the neighbor's yard when you're ready for Frisbee."

"Okay," I say.

We spent last fall by the neighbor's yard where there's more room to practice and he'd be out there every day, pitching to me. I never thanked him for that. He turns and leaves so abrupt it almost ruins the moment but it's okay. This is so strange either way and I sink back into the shadows away from the party. Naruto never dealt with coming out to his father.

I close my eyes again, wiping the sweat from my forehead. I think I fall asleep.

※

"Matty?"

I'm definitely asleep.

"You in there?"

It's Titi, snaking her head through the opening—curly black hair wrapped in a bun atop her head.

"Yeah." I open my eyes and squint in the light.

"There's someone here to see you."

She spins and waves him in and then he's standing here, in front of me, and Titi keeps speaking but I can't hear what she's saying.

"I saw him walking out to Route 35 and I thought it was you for a second—you both have those T-shirts with that weird band name."

He's hiding his face like he's afraid to face me.

"And I wanted to drive him to the hospital but he said he needed to see you first and he wouldn't listen so I brought him here."

Stick looks up for half a second, the sun at the side of his face. His nose is swollen, and his left eye is shut, puffing out at the bottom with blackened veins across his cheek.

"Hey."

I don't recognize his voice, I don't recognize his face, his hair is a swirl of knotted black and brown and his eyes are sunken in.

"Matt's mom has a first aid kit inside," Titi says, "but we should really get you to a hospital."

"Thanks," Stick says, but his voice is slurred, or maybe just jumbled in my head. "I need to talk to Matt."

Titi looks from Stick to me and I wish for once in my life I knew what the fuck was happening.

"I'll go get some ice," she says. "Matt, keep an eye on him, please."

"Okay," I say, or I think I say, I might have only nodded or not responded at all, watching the wide smear of blood seep down his cheek, all the way to his chin. I step aside and offer him a seat as he limps over to me.

"What happened?"

I stand back to give him some room, the salsa blaring in the distance.

"My mom."

"She hit you?"

"No, I would have slapped that bitch right back," he says, the anger fixing his speech. "I came downstairs this morning and she yelled at me for not coming home last night."

He shakes his head and winces, the scarring already starting beneath the welt around his eye. His nose looks broken.

"So I yelled back, I told her everything I'd been holding back and all of a sudden her asshole boyfriend comes into the kitchen and he gets all loud and I just—I lost it, Matt, I fucking lost it on him—"

"You hit him?"

"Yeah. I mean I kind of took a swing and he ducked and it hit him on the shoulder then he was about to hit me back but Mom—she jumped in between us to keep us apart and I was trying to get back at him and then I feel these hands yanking me away from her and out of the kitchen down into the garage."

His left eye starts flickering, the blood caked onto the lid.

"David and Marcus," Stick says. "They said I hit Mom and maybe I did, I was trying to get at her boyfriend and they wouldn't let me explain what happened so I called them fucking assholes for defending that bitch and they held me down and beat the shit out of me."

"Oh my god," I say as Stick catches his breath. The swelling keeps mounting around his eye.

"Yeah." The music is louder again, and Nico is screaming outside the fence. I wonder where Titi went for the ice because Stick is still bleeding.

"I ran out of the garage and called Sherry. They're down at the shore but when they get back, they're coming for me," he says. "I'm not going back to that house."

"No," I say, "you can't."

"I just started walking, I don't know where I was going," he says. "I didn't think I could come here. I wouldn't have come here but your aunt, she—"

He reaches up to his eye and winces again.

"She's getting you ice." I look back for Titi but Stick pulls at my cast.

"Matt?"

It hurts, everything hurts, but his eye is fully closed, and his cheek is twice the size of a normal cheek.

"What happened to your lip?"

"It's nothing." He's looking at me, his face more broken than mine. "When I fell off the bed before you left," I say.

"Shit."

"It's okay." I don't want to relive last night right now. Ever.

"It's not okay. Shit."

"I'm fine," I say. "I mean, forget it." I want to forget it.

"No, Matt, it's just … fuck …" He shakes his head and winces. "I shouldn't have left like that. I just—I freaked out—and I know that keeps happening and I shouldn't have said what I said I … I'm just so angry lately. I'm angry all the time."

Tears start to mix with the blood on his face and I want to reach out to touch but I'm afraid. And I can't forgive him this time.

"What happened in here?"

I turn and see Willie limping across the broken concrete into the shed. Titi pushes around him, placing the bag of ice on Stick's face. His left eye is closed completely.

"I said 'what happened'?" Willie says. "And don't bullshit me. No one got time for that."

He's speaking to Stick, and I don't know if they've ever met but he somehow knows to answer.

"I got in a fight," Stick says.

"Nope. Did I not just say I got no time for bullshit," Willie says, legs bowed as he steps closer to Stick. "Who beat you?"

Stick hesitates, looking to me, but I nod for him to tell Uncle Willie what he needs to know.

"My brothers," Stick says.

"Does your father know about this?"

Stick drops his head, pulling the ice away, and Titi explains about the funeral.

"Okay, okay, I'm sorry to hear that," Willie says, then smacks me in the shoulder. "Does your father know?"

I shake my head. "No."

"I'll be back," Willie says and shuffles out of the shed.

Titi returns the ice to Stick's face and repeats her demand that we head to the hospital. Stick says he can't—he says they'll notify the police and Marcus has an arrest record and even though he hates him they're still family but I don't know why he's defending him. Dad comes in through the opening to the shed.

"Who did this?" he says.

Stick looks over to me again. Willie is standing behind him.

"Stick, which brothers did this?"

"David and Marcus," he says.

"The ones in the garage always smoking pot?"

Stick nods. Dad doesn't like Stick's brothers, I'm not sure he even likes Stick, but ever since his father died, when we'd drive by and see the door open, David and Marcus would always be smoking and I'd have to convince Dad not to stop the car and yell, like a father yells, now that their father is gone.

"I figured." He steps back out of the door with Willie. "We'll take care of it."

"What are you going to do?" Titi asks.

"We'll have a talk with them," Dad says. "Family or not, you don't beat your little brother like that. They need to know."

"Wait—Jay—don't make it worse," Titi says.

"We got it," Willie says. "Ain't your concern. We're just having a chat with these boys. Ain't nothin' you need to worry about."

"No, please," Stick says, attempting to stand. "Marcus is legit crazy. He can't control himself."

"Well if they get crazy, we'll get crazy right back," Willie says, and I see one of my aluminum bats in his lowered hand. I look at Titi because this shit is escalating way too fast and it's all my fault, Stick would have come home with me if I didn't touch him in Teddy's bedroom.

Titi nods and follows them out of the shed and I hope she can help but I doubt they'll listen. My dad never listens. I guess it's kind of cool that he's defending Stick—it's like he's defending me by proxy, but he has to know it won't help, nothing will help. My head starts spinning and I feel like I'm falling, bracing myself against the walls of the shed but it won't stop, it doesn't stop. I look over to Stick and his face is covered in ice.

I shouldn't, I know I shouldn't, but it's not his fault that his family life is fucked, and I want to forgive him. I want to save him. Still. And I hate that we're breaking—everything is broken—I didn't want to come out like this and I didn't want to be broken like this and I didn't want Dad to go have a fight with Stick's brothers, I didn't want any of this. I only wanted Stick.

"What are they going to do?" he says.

My head keeps spinning—like really fucking spinning—like I need to lie down and sleep for twenty-four hours straight but it's so hot out here and Stick's still bleeding and I still want to love him like I've always loved him.

"Matt?" he says. "What's happening?"

He reaches out for me and I want him to touch, like last night under the covers, smashing our lips together. I recoil at the touch.

His broken face looks up at me, the sun at my back spreading heat through my cheeks and spilling my chakra onto the hot concrete. I can't watch him break.

So I run. I break into a sprint out the shed through the gate, Nico screaming from the side but growing distant. I pick up speed away from the house and away from my family, away from the salsa blaring unnecessarily and everyone celebrating while Stick is in the shed breaking.

I will not be okay.

I don't know how I convinced myself I would.

TWENTY-SIX

EXPLOSIONS IN THE SKY bursting with the sound and all these echoing vibrations rattling through the field beneath us, Stick and me side by side in the wet tall grass with the bugs and the heat and our sweat, on vacation, the end of our vacation, Stick at my side watching explosions in the sky, one at a time then in a sweltering rush, everything so rushed in my mind with this high and these thick jolting booms crashing through every second with a flash in the distance screaming darkness like I'm dreaming, broken dreaming, half asleep and broken in half it seems, Stick gone from my side with his legs splayed over mine, all the lights burning bright and then breaking, flitting fading, until I forget they were here and now they're gone.

We used to go to the high school to see the fireworks, my mom and the teachers from her school with their kids, these chattering girls and smelly boys who wouldn't bother with me or I wouldn't bother with them, maybe because I liked them. Stick and me are sort of wet and nearly rusting almost molting from the heat of his body wedged beneath my body, under the covers in Teddy's spare bedroom, wide awake and escaping, flitting fading, more perfect than perfect but now it's gone.

I haven't slept so I might be seeing things, images in the distance like Stick chasing after me, past the row of trees at the edge of our development. I want to sleep but I can't fall asleep, it's like I'm wide awake and dreaming but I don't remember dreaming, I don't remember anything but Stick and me in Teddy's bedroom, and I close my eyes to find Stick's face inside, his lips on my lips, his fingers touching mine. He says he doesn't love me, or he can't and he won't. I watched Dad's car drive down the street to Stick's house. I keep my eyes closed.

Stick, can I ask you something?

He swipes his hair left to right like he always does, the sweat matting down against the skin.

When you're with Staci, I mean—do you think about me?

Of course, he says with a sick, winking smile. I smile back.

The colors are brighter now, harder and sharper, so the images blur and the sounds get obscured, loud enough to hear but not quite place the song. I want to sink down and hide but there's nowhere to hide and the heat in this field is piercing my skin until it's beginning again, that nauseating feeling that pops right in, the lights so bright I can't see again. We won't ever kiss again.

No one needs to know, I say. We can keep it like a secret.

We tried that. Your mom found out.

She won't say anything. My parents are cool with it, I think. It's weird.

You told your parents?

His voice is louder now, not so far in the distance, this sudden buzzing scraping into my mind like I'm dreaming, sleeping dreaming, and I can't wake up because I'm not asleep and all this clattering is cracking at my skull—seeping in through the folds of gray matter, the rattling of the train on the tracks through the trees, as Stick shifts forward, sweeping his hair left to right, his skin wet with sweat and eyes wide open, kissing me. I open my eyes to find him standing there. I will be okay.

"Stick?"

"You mind if I sit?"

"No." I reach up to wipe my eyes.

"I figured you'd be here," he says, squatting down on the grass. "I guess I know you pretty well."

His left eye is open again, the icepack effective enough to get the swelling down a bit. The train's horn bellows in the distance. He curls his feet underneath.

"Your mom is looking for you. She said you won't answer your phone."

I fish it out from deep in my pocket to find the thirty-eight messages she's sent since I left the house. Titi must have told her what's happening.

"This is all such a mess," Stick says.

I don't look at him. I don't know what to say.

"I'm moving in with Sherry," he says.

His face is bruised beneath the eye but not nearly as swollen and the blood is cleaned up, his nose only one-and-a-half times bigger than normal.

"When?"

"Pretty much now," he says. "I mean, when she comes to pick me up."

"But I thought there wasn't any room at her house?"

"There isn't. But I can't go home. I called her again and they're heading back from the shore to get me."

He looks out to the street so I can't see his eyes, just the back of his head and his hair, losing its color with the summer now over. He's leaving me.

"So that's it," I say.

"What?"

"You're leaving?"

"I have to," he says. "I mean, I'm staying at Sherry's until we figure it out about the custody, but I can't stay at the house with my brothers."

"Does Sherry even live in Woodbridge?"

"No. But it's not that far. And I'll still go to Woodbridge High. They don't need to know I moved."

He winces as he squints, reaching for his side. Stick never stayed over my house this summer.

"But you are moving."

"Yeah."

I'm an asshole. His whole world has fallen apart—way worse than mine, like infinitely worse, and all I can think is he's leaving me. Again.

"I'm sorry," I say.

"For what?"

I look down at my wrist, itching worse without sleep and I kind of want to cut off the cast, straight to the bone just to get some relief. I don't know if it'll ever feel the same again.

"I haven't been there for you when you needed me."

"Yes, you have," Stick says. "You totally have, you have no idea."

"No. I haven't. Not really."

He reaches out and grabs my hand, the good hand, squeezing tight. It doesn't hurt anymore, it's just numb.

"Would you stop? I should be apologizing to you—I'm the one who—" He shakes his head and slams his fist into the grass. "I started kissing you and then I freaked out and said we couldn't be friends. I'm the one who's a horrible friend and I keep being a horrible friend and here you are apologizing to me."

"I'm sorry."

"See!" He laughs. I didn't mean to make him laugh. "Before I called Sherry this morning, you know what my first thought was—the only thought I had since I left Asbury actually—it was you. I didn't think of Janice or Sherry or Staci—oh god not Staci, it was you, Matt. It's always been you. I thought you would hate me."

I laugh. I didn't mean to laugh. "I thought you said you knew me."

"What?"

"You know I can't hate you."

I love you.

I don't say it because I don't know how to say it and I know I shouldn't be thinking it, but I've given up trying to control my mind. I squeeze his hand pretty tight. He lets me.

"Yeah, I know," Stick says, both eyes fully open. "And I was wrong. Nothing needs to change. We can hang out in school and I'll bike over after school every day and have Sherry pick me up and we'll forget what I said last night, that was me being crazy."

My grip is so tight I can't feel my skin.

"You're my best friend. I can't lose you."

"Just friends then?" It slips right out but it's all up in my head and I can't get it out. How much I love him. He needs to know.

"I didn't say that." My grip eases a bit. His face is raw and dark. "You know, when I was like seven or eight and Sherry was dating Pat, I didn't really know what it meant when she got engaged—I just thought that Pat would move in with us and nothing would change, you know?" He releases my hand and I glance down the street. Dad and Willie haven't driven back but I haven't been looking. "So we all got dressed up for the wedding and I was wearing this little suit, one of Jarrett's old ones I think, because he used to be little like me and we were sitting in the pews and I think I asked Janice which room they were moving into—Sherry and Pat— and she laughed and told me that Sherry was moving out. And it killed me, you know, I just started crying right there in church, like I never really cried before. And I know it's stupid, but Mom she just—she never really mothered me, even when I was a kid, it was Sherry who watched me every night and she used to let me sleep in her bed. She'd read me the same book every time—this really old Disney book but I wouldn't let her switch no matter how often she tried."

His eyes are cloudy and the sun is bright on his face.

"And I realize now I was being selfish, but she left me, that's all I thought at the time, and I wouldn't forgive her, not for a while. And I hated Pat, I would be so mean to him at their apartment, like really mean, he probably still hates me for that. No way he wants me to move in."

He laughs again and it makes me smile. I don't know why but I smile.

"Aileen got married next and the rest of the older kids, they all left and then Mom, which—yeah, I'm not going to forgive her for that—but then Dad, fucking Dad of all people." He looks back to the street, shielding his eyes from me. "You know where he had the heart attack?"

I shake my head. He's not looking.

"He got home from work and he was sitting in our driveway. The car was still running, and he collapsed, right on the front seat. David found him but we don't know how long he was out, just that they couldn't wake him up and the ambulance came, and he never woke up again."

He's crying. I reach out to hug him and he lets me hug him, this deep long embrace, perfect and strange, and for a second it flashes that maybe Puerto Ricans have a point because I never had a hug feel better than this.

"I don't want you to leave me, Matt. I think that scares me more than being gay even. I mean, what if we tried dating again and it got too hard and we stopped speaking, you know? What if I lost you, too?"

"You won't," I say. I need him to believe me.

"I like you, Matt. A lot. And I don't even know what that means but I never felt like this about anyone before and definitely not a boy and it scares the shit out of me, not just because you're a guy but I think about you all the time and I—" He bites his lips to stop them from shaking. "I don't know why I'm so afraid of this."

I reach out again and he looks up, his watery eyes and broken nose, hesitating because I'm not moving and then he's half-crying, half-laughing when he jerks me into him and kisses me again. And it hurts—like there's this physical pain on my lips but it doesn't matter, nothing matters but this.

"Sorry," he says, touching my swollen lips. He smiles and leans forward again.

"Wait," I say. "What is this?"

"What do you mean?"

"Like—" I make a motion back and forth between us, indicating this back and forth between us.

"I don't know, Matt," he says. "I really don't. I mean, we could do another trial, if you want. I think I'd like that."

"No," I say. I need to say it. "No more trials. It needs to be for real this time. That's what we both want, isn't it?"

"Yeah," Stick says and he leans back for a second. Longer than a second. "But I still can't figure out how that would work. I mean—I can't come out. Not yet. I'm not ready for that, I don't even know if I'm ..."

He trails off and another train is approaching.

"You don't have to come out," I say. "We can take it super slow. And now that my parents know, we can at least be cool around the house."

"Wait—what?"

The train picks up speed and I think maybe I forgot to tell him that I CAME OUT TO MY PARENTS THIS MORNING. I think that's what happened. I'm not sure this isn't all a dream.

"I told them. They were grilling me about my lip and coming home so late so yeah ... they know. And so does Cara and probably Kepler at this point. I'm just coming out all over the place today."

"Jesus."

The rumbling on the tracks is getting louder and I can't read Stick's face or I'm afraid to read it, I love him more than anything and I don't want to hide it. I want this to be for real. There's a chance this can be real.

"What did your dad say?"

"He's okay with it, I think. He wasn't angry. And he asked me to play Frisbee. So that was weird."

Stick smiles and looks out past the field toward his house. The train passes by too loud for us to speak.

"Stick, I'm gay and my parents know and I'm okay with that. I can't believe I'm saying it but I'm okay with it and I'm here for you no matter what, if you just want to be friends again, or coming out. But I need to know what you're thinking because I think I love you."

I focus on my feet, the spiky grass sticking up underneath, and I know I went too far, but I need to know for sure and Stick isn't speaking. The train cruises past my development.

"I can't believe your dad went over to beat up my brothers."

He laughs, but I'm not sure why. I look hard at him, waiting.

"I'm totally jealous of your family, Matt."

"Why?"

"Just like, the way they stick up for you," he says. "Or for me, I mean. I don't know, you know I love your mom." He pauses long enough to throw in a wink, from the eye not battered and swollen. "Not like that—"

I try not to, but I can't help but smile. He shifts closer and touches my side.

"It's just that her son, you know, he's my best friend and he's really fucking cool and he's also really hot and I don't know what to do with that."

He squeezes my leg and it snakes through my skin.

"Don't be gay," I say.

He laughs, fully now, then he reaches around me and pulls my face into his face, my lips into his lips. The perfect kiss. His cheek is swollen and the red is burnt into his skin. I pull back.

"What's wrong?" he says. I need him to say it.

"No trial, just dating. This needs to be for real, okay?"

"Okay," he says and it spikes through my head, these explosions so bright I can't even see the sky this time. I steady myself with my cast on the grass and we kiss again. It's perfect.

"Matt." He pulls back, finding my eyes. "Thank you."

"For what?"

"For this."

The smile spreads across his face, shiny and broken and perfect.

"Always," I say.

I will be okay. EVERYTHING.

※

Acknowledgements

First and foremost, I need to acknowledge the two families that made this story possible. My own family—especially Mom and Dad—thanks for your unwavering support, both in writing and in life. And to Elba and Figgy and your wonderful family, thank you for welcoming me into your lives and giving me love and acceptance.

To Tanya, thank you for the many, many years of friendship and for allowing me to become part of your family, the experiences of which contributed to the joys present in Mateo's close-knit family. And to Mike, who never likes all the hours I spend writing because it keeps us apart, but if it weren't for him, Stick and his family would have never been realized on the pages of this novel and I truly appreciate all the love you've given me throughout this process.

To Jackie, who has always been my biggest writing booster, thank you for your great advice and support. To Laura, for all her writing advice and all the happy hours at Treehouse and the fact that she still became my friend after I rooted through her purse on the first night we hung out. To the New School writing group who provided invaluable feedback, particularly those that became my closest friends in NYC—Katie, Kat, Alex, and dear departed Jodi. To the fellow Rowan writers who read a super early and very different draft of this story a decade ago. And to my writing professors, thank you for all your knowledge and encouragement, in particular Julia Chang, Jen Courtney, Carla Spataro, John Reed, and the late Denise Gess.

To my wonderful editor Kristy Makansi and the rest of my publishing team at Amphorae (Lisa Miller and Laura Robinson), thanks for getting this out into the world. To my agent Veronica Park at Fuse Literary, thank you for connecting me with Amphorae and for all of your support in getting my writing published now and in the future. To The World is a Beautiful Place and I Am No Longer Afraid to Die, thank you for letting me use your lyrics in this story and for serving as inspiration for Mateo & Stick, and of course, for all the great shows. We will all be okay.

And finally, to the friends who supported me throughout this process—Karen, Rob, Jonathan, Matt, Larry, Jill, Andrea, Aaron, Crystal, Michael, Murph, Gina, Felipe, Rich Sr., Rich, and Lauren (who helped me with the limited Spanish in this book, it's her fault if it's wrong!). And of course to Elie, the newest joy in my life. For everything.

About the Author

Bill Elenbark started writing stories in the empty pages of engineering class notebooks in massive lecture halls at Rutgers University. He earned his MA in Writing at Rowan University where his love for Young Adult stories flourished. He is an avid indie rock music fan who has attended close to 500 shows over the past decade, from the "do it yourself" spaces of Brooklyn to landmark stages in Los Angeles and New York City. He travels all across the country for his day job as an engineer and has lived all over the state of New Jersey. When he's home he spends much of his time commuting to coffee shops in Manhattan and Brooklyn to write. He once had an active baseball life in little league and middle school but gave it up after a frightening inability to hit a curve ball. He currently resides with his boyfriend in Hoboken. This is his first novel.